The Gold *of* the North

Also by Joan H. Parks

The Late Bronze Age Stories:
    Thutmose
    Lukenow
    Petros
    The Bedouin
    Dalil

Contemporary Stories:
    The Book Club Chronicles
    The Book Club Chronicles, Part Two
    The Book Club Chronicles, Part Three
    The Book Club Chronicles, Part Four - Macbeth

Memoir:
    32 Linden Avenue

The Gold of the North

PART SIX OF THE LATE BRONZE AGE STORIES

JOAN H. PARKS

THE GOLD OF THE NORTH

iUniverse books may be ordered through booksellers or by contacting:

iUniverse
1663 Liberty Drive
Bloomington, IN 47403
www.iuniverse.com
1-800-Authors (1-800-288-4677)

Because of the dynamic nature of the Internet, any web addresses or links contained in this book may have changed since publication and may no longer be valid. The views expressed in this work are solely those of the author and do not necessarily reflect the views of the publisher, and the publisher hereby disclaims any responsibility for them.

Any people depicted in stock imagery provided by Thinkstock are models, and such images are being used for illustrative purposes only. Certain stock imagery © Thinkstock.

ISBN: 978-1-4917-8117-3 (sc)
ISBN: 978-1-4917-8118-0 (e)

Library of Congress Control Number: 2015917702

Print information available on the last page.

iUniverse rev. date: 10/24/2015

CONTENTS

HISTORICAL NOTE

The sea peoples menaced the eastern coast of the Mediterranean during the late Bronze Age. The movement of tribes and peoples has left a confusing and scant archeological record. The palace cultures of Minos, and most of the cities along the Mediterranean were destroyed—by whom is still a matter of conjecture. Egypt barely escaped and the destruction did not extend to Mesopotamia. Ugarit, a port city (present day Syria) where the trade routes for Crete, Cyprus, Egypt, Mesopotamia and Afghanistan converged, was destroyed in 1190 BCE and never rebuilt. The remains were found by accident in 1929 and archeological excavations have continued except when interrupted by war, so that maps of the city now exist. Cuneiform tablets were found in the oven during excavations. Whether it was internal corruption, changing climate that provoked tribes to move, or technological advances in weaponry that caused the destruction is still hotly argued in books and articles.

Between Egypt, Mesopotamia and Scandinavia: Late Bronze Age glass beads found in Denmark: Varberg, J; Gratuze, B; Kaul, F. Journal of Archeological Science: Vol 54, 168-81, 2015

Chapter One

Alimah Is Alone

I know not when or if I shall ever see them again. I could run after them, crying "Wait, wait! I will go with you!" It is not too late. But I do nothing. I can do nothing.

Kaliq does not look back as he rides away from me. He and Petros the Wise and the Bedouin and Dalil become smaller and smaller until they vanish in the distance. Dust stirred up from their departure settles into its usual pattern. All is quiet under the implacable sun. I am left with my kin who are new to me.

I seek out the war mare whom I have ridden from the time we left the kin on the ancient trade route. I rode her on the long trails that lead to the Great Green Sea. I rode her as bandits attacked us. I rode her along that sea until we reached our destination: The Land of the One River and our blood relatives whom Bakiri leads. I rode her that day when the Evil One's men tried to capture me. She fought as I fought that day, with wild resolve.

The mare nuzzles my hair, blowing her warm breath on me. I wrap my arms around her supple neck, press my face against her warm body and let my tears flow. She patiently awaits my revival.

I ride in the hot wind—the hot wind that dries my tears. Alone with the one live being from my home and my long journey, my heart quiets.

Chapter Two

Alimah tries to Understand Her Story

My own mother told me that I sang and danced as soon as I climbed to my feet. I made up songs, and tried to sound like the tuneful birds that inhabited where we lived. I did not yet grasp that the birds of the air used their songs to fight for territory, to sing to their mates, and to protect their young.

I moved my body in dances as soon as I could—as soon as my body obeyed what I saw so clearly in my mind, and felt so strongly in my limbs. I dimly remember those early times when I had to sing and dance as much as I had to breathe and eat to keep my body alive.

I know that as long as I have enough strength in me to live, I will need to make songs and bring them to others to hear, to make dances for others to see. I have known that from the earliest times. It is no different now. I seek to make my songs more beautiful. My fingers caress the stringed boxes to draw out the music that is locked in them, until

3

I set it free. I seek to free the enchanted sounds from the reeds with my lips and my breath, as I had seen done by the ones trained in the art. I need to see how the music-making devices are made and perhaps persuade one of the clever ones who make them to bring his talents to my people. I need to study the movements of the dance that are new to me here in the Land of the One River. No matter how awkward I am as I learn, learn I must.

My mother and father thought I was too young to go on the long journey to the Land of the One River. Once they knew that Serena would be one of the travelling ones, they relaxed, but I noticed that they each, singly, had intense words with Serena and with Petros the Wise, her brother. I was not to know what those words were, for I was imagined to be too much the child to be made aware of the perils to which I would soon be exposed.

I chafed at being thought a child. I had long since known that my great gifts set me apart from the other children. Visitors to the kin had looked at me since I was very small, and lately, as I was growing into my womanly body, I had become aware of the different looks on men's faces—some had speculative looks as when seeing a particularly fine war mare. Others had the hot look of desire. I took care to never be alone with them.

On the journey, my kin protected me. Serena took me under her care and taught me much about the looks of men that we encountered along the long journey to the Land of the One River. She, who had the gift of songs, protected me, taught me how to obey orders that kept me safe. With danger surrounding us, I was no longer permitted to roam free as I had when growing up with the kin.

We made our way along the dusty trails, mounted on the fleet and nimble war mares that The Bedouin provided. Along the ancient trade route that led to the Great Green Sea, common bandits tried to deprive us of our war mares and any other valuable goods. From the remains of Ugarit along the Great Green Sea, we set out to the Land of the One River to be with Bakiri, our blood relative who bred and protected the war mares. Along this route villains lurked to deprive us of the war mares and our very lives.

A bitter ruined woman, a remote descendant of Thutmose, our revered ancestor, was the source of the evil that reached out to the ends of the trade route to harm us and almost succeeded in sending Dalil to be with his ancestors. The blood feud was a great danger to our newfound kin in the Land of The One River, for the woman lived near them and used her band of drugged servants as a constant threat. Even after so long that none remained to remember the living Thutmose, the rage did not subside but grew in fierceness.

Petros the Wise and the rest of our elders decided it was our duty to destroy the Evil Ones, to destroy utterly the serpents in their nest so they could menace us no more. That decision was made even before we left where our kin made their home. All that was in doubt was the source of the evil. It was worse than the elders had thought, for the Evil One used the red seeds from the Land of the Bull Dancers to enslave and cloud the minds of all who were within her sway. She could not be allowed to live, for her power was growing and was a danger to all those among whom she lived.

Serena was captured, along with The Bedouin, by the Evil One. In a long ago time, now embedded in the stories of the kin, Serena had been captured and Petros had rescued her. Yet again, Petros the Wise plotted to free his sister. This time, our enemies tried to capture me too, but Kaliq scooped me off my war mare and, clasping me tightly to him, swiftly returned me to safety amidst the sounds of yelling men, clashing daggers, and the pounding hooves of the war mares.

After the Evil One was destroyed, Kaliq and I had long, sun-filled days to know more of each other. He would return after seeing hard sights and his heart lightened at hearing my songs, or even just sitting and talking with me. My very being went out to him. The more I knew of him, the more I knew that I wished to spend my life with him. My heart opened to him after his daring rescue. His clever actions in reaching Serena and The Bedouin in their captivity made him renowned among the warriors. All thought it fitting that Kaliq studied with Petros the Wise to refine his natural talents as a leader.

Yet something held me back from pledging myself to Kaliq, which I understood not. He, at times, looked hurt or puzzled, but I could not ease that hurt or tell him what stopped me from pledging myself to him. My tongue would not say the words.

The turmoil was such that it took all of my strength to decline to make the long journey with him to rejoin our kin. I found it hard to say no, but could not say yes. The look on Kaliq's face as he bent over my hands saying farewell tore at me. I looked the other way. If I had said yes to him, by our traditions, I would not have been able to explore the new ways that the Land of the One River provided for me. I would have returned to be with him, be his mate and make my life with him.

Not yet. It is not yet the time for mating with him. I need to perfect my gifts for song and dance. If I follow my heart, then my very self would be diminished; the Alimah who did that would not be the Alimah who I wished to be— who I know I can be. Perhaps I would not be the Alimah that Kaliq desired, but the mere outward form. My people have many gifted ones among us and understand what I need, what drives me. All understand that I need to sing and dance or something within me will die.

Here, in the Land of the One River, was what might be my one chance to study new ways of song and the dance. If I do not stay, my gift will be weakened. I am one of the gifted who must follow my own path or I will be of no use to myself or those whom I love. Sardow, another of Petros the Wise's sisters, was one of the gifted. She loved, but knew that if she did not remain with her people her gift would be squandered. So she stayed, and that she died too soon did not make her decision flawed.

I could have asked Serena for advice for she was wise. I did not. I need to follow my own instincts, without hearing the voices that could disturb my inner clarity. So I remain quiet.

Bakiri, our kinsman who will be my protector in the time ahead, glances at me. To my surprise, I realize that not only does he look like Petros the Wise but that he also thinks like him. He is not one of the gifted ones and at one time did not understand them. Bakiri has learned much since Salama, a gifted one under his protection, had to flee from The Land of the One River. He is trying to use the same light touch he uses with the war mares to handle the much more intricate, human gifted ones who come under his protection.

In the midst of my own turmoil at saying goodbye to Kaliq and all those with whom I have been living for many moons, I almost smile to myself at the thought that I will be teaching Bakiri how to nourish the gifted ones. Maybe that is how I can be of use to him, to repay him for his protection.

I stop that thought for it is the destiny of the protectors to protect, with no thought of paying back. They must protect just as I must learn and sing the songs and perhaps make up my own. My own songs have been gathering force inside of me, gathering force to where I need to open my mouth and let them out: songs to enchant, songs to entertain, songs to make the hearers weep or laugh or sigh in contentment. All these songs are welling up inside of me, waiting for me to let them loose to live in their most perfect form.

Chapter Three

Bakiri and Alimah Make Plans

"Alimah, I have found the place that teaches dance and music."

"Thank you, Uncle." I call him "Uncle," a term of respect.

Bakiri and I stand at the pasture, each putting one foot up on the fence as we study the war mares. Sand covers this part of the pasture, so the war mares can roll in it, their delicate legs waving in the air. Cavorting and running in the sand strengthens their legs. Another pasture, green with young grass, beckons them to come and feed. It beckons us with its sweet growing scent and its vivid colors. Dull sand and green crops: that to me is the Land of the One River.

This is where the men go to talk—standing at the fence, looking at the war mares and sharing their thoughts, their problems and their solutions. Looking at the lovely creatures seems to soothe them.

We hear the distant sounds of the women cooking, and the children squealing at some game they are playing. The boys will be playing war games, and replaying the late war that was only too real. The girls will be playing at cooking and taking care of babies. In the midst of this are the sounds of chickens scratching in the dust, goats bleating as they wander through the open spaces and the lowing of the cattle waiting to be led to the river as the day ends. All will leave and take the donkeys and the other animals down to the river as the day starts to wane and the night approaches.

Bakiri smiles at me. "I know nothing of dance, and what is good and what is not. I know nothing of song and the instruments that make pleasing sounds. The war mares I know about, but not these arts. I have asked those who know of such things and they all agreed on this one place. But, sometimes all agree on how to train the war mares and they are, each and every one, wrong in what they think. The choice will be yours, for Petros the Wise and Serena believe that, as a part of your gift, you will be aware of what is the best."

I am curious as to what Serena and Petros the Wise said to him. I look at him, the question on my lips. He sees and answers before the words lay on the air.

"Serena told me to trust your eye. We will see the school and watch the pupils. Perhaps you can teach me to tell the gifted from the not gifted."

I look at him in surprise. He is going to come with me and not just hand me over to one of the women? Or one of his sons? He is taking this very seriously. Then I think again. From the time I was very small, men's eyes have followed me, have been drawn to me. Some made me very uneasy. Serena

10

told me that Sardow was the same. Serena taught me to gauge those looks and how dangerous they might be, or not be. She taught me to be self-possessed and not to respond to remarks made to me. She taught me the lessons she learned as a young girl: how to disguise herself and make herself invisible when her safety depended upon it. She taught me, that when I have great need to be unnoticed or to divert attention from myself, to garb myself as a boy and walk or swagger as a boy moves. Sardow, Serena's sister, garbed herself as a boy, and carried a dagger which she knew how to use. I carry a dagger, too, given to me by Serena who taught me how to use it. I carry several daggers about my person, some so cleverly disguised that they look not like weapons.

Bakiri, in coming with me to see the dancers and singers, is letting others know that I am under his protection—that I am of worth. I wonder if this will draw enemies to me or if it will help protect me.

We leave the next morning, for there is no sense in delaying. Bakiri, as is proper, issues the orders for all of us to follow. I have learned to not question orders in my journey from the land of my kin to where I am today. Serena explained that my very life and the lives of my protectors depended upon my following orders exactly, so I have ceased childish questioning.

"Stay close to me on the road," Bakiri says. "Do not wander. We, even although a small group, are well protected. The trails and roads were once safe for a solitary traveler, but are no longer safe. Since the Great Destruction, nothing is as it was. Where once Pharaoh's soldiers kept order with their chariots patrolling the lanes and roads, sometimes now they prey on those they should protect."

Bakiri draws in a breath. "We have always had to protect the war mares from the greed of those in power, but now we have to be wary of all whom we meet on a journey." He looked down at me. "Was it like this for you on the way to the Great Green Sea and then down the coast to my land?"

I reply, "Yes, Bakiri. It was never safe. I was trained to be wary of all strangers, for they most likely were our enemies."

Bakiri looks at me with raised eyebrows. "I notice that you obey instantly those who protect us."

"Serena and Petros the Wise taught me," I say.

"The worst of men roam the roads, seizing what they have the strength to seize. They have none to be loyal to; they have no women or children to protect. They scavenge like the feral dogs that cannot be trusted," he continues sadly.

Bakiri's mouth tightens at the changes in his land. His is a face that was meant to be genial, but I have seen the grey creep into his hair and the lines deepen around his mouth since first I met him.

Sternly, he says to all of us, "I choose our most valiant young warriors to go with us. We have one of my sons who has learned much from our late troubles. We have some of the young warriors whom Petros the Wise left here to learn of the Land of the One River. The war mares and fine linens that we wear attract those who would take them from us. We have enough well-armed young men to discourage casual villains but not enough to provoke fear amongst those who are powerful in this area. The message we send walks a fine line for those with the wits to read it."

Bakiri shows no fear, but only an increasing wariness at the dangers that may come upon us unannounced on this journey. The young warriors respect his leadership, for he earned that respect as he was tested in the late war with the Evil One.

I put aside the wrench of the departure of the travelers, of those whom I have shared so much. I put aside any fears that might arise about the dangers that might come to us. I can only think about worthy teachers whom I can learn from.

Off we ride in the dust and the early morning heat. The yellow, glowing sun makes its way above the hills, tingeing the dark blue with streaks of pink and orange. The great river sparkles in the distance. Donkeys bray, chickens scratch in the dust, birds flit overhead. Our war mares toss their heads joyfully and prance down the dusty trail, their tails arched and flowing.

For the moment, all is well.

Chapter Four

Bakiri and Alimah Inspect the School

There is no need to rush so we take our time, stopping at inns along the way, where Bakiri and his son are well known. Such is the turmoil from the Great Destruction that all who live here need to trade news about which bands of landless men are armed and dangerous and which ones are desperate and dangerous. Outsiders are looked at with suspicion because of the dangers that come with them.

I am stared at, but it does not make me uneasy, for Bakiri is not uneasy. The inns provide us with food and talk. Strangers are not welcome for they steal food and drink and anything else they can. Bakiri is known and trusted. He trades talk with the others there, seemingly casually but I can tell from the sharp look in his eyes that he is alert to small bits of rumor that would make him familiar with new quarrels and alliances where we are headed. He finds out which trails and roads are secure and which are not. It will take much longer to reach our destination than we had planned.

Even though we take the safer routes, we are beset by those who appear suddenly, ready to destroy us. I have become used to violence. I am shielded from harm by a circle of young warriors, whilst the others use swords and cudgels to disarm those who try to harm us. No longer am I shocked by the bodies that are left by the trail. If those who attack us had had their way, it would have been our bodies left to rot in the hot sun, a feast for the ever present vultures. I hope that I am not becoming numb to the suffering to which I am a reluctant witness.

"We live in a constant state of war." Bakiri says softly one morning as we ride on. I wonder again if I should have gone back with Kaliq and the rest of the kin who live beyond where the Great Destruction has ravaged the land. My needs might be exposing these fine men to dangers that are unnecessary. Every day we see more signs of the turmoil that has been brought to this rich land. Those in small villages, when first they see our troop, look fearful and only calm down when they become aware that we mean them no harm and, indeed, can provide protection while we are with them.

Several weary days later we reach our destination, the home of one of Bakiri's fellow men of the horse. At our host's compound are the familiar pastures that hold sleek and happy war mares. I am welcomed by the women and shown into a small room where I will keep my few belongings. I expect to live at the school while I learn, so I pay scant attention to that small room, thinking that I will only sleep in it the one night. The next day we will go to the school that Bakiri has found and, if all goes well, I will say another good bye and be on my own, with no one I know.

These friends of Bakiri breed the war mares and try to keep them out of the hands of Pharaoh's army, where their lives would be wasted in useless wars. I suspect but do not know that Bakiri and his friends, the people of the horse, have secluded spots where they hide their best stallions and their best war mares. I also suspect that they know when Pharaoh's soldiers will arrive to take the war mares and that they will hide the best ones from their sight. None of this I know, but I have heard snatches of the talk between Bakiri and Petros the Wise, and have seen how Petros's eyes gleam as he laughs and says, "Very clever, Bakiri, very clever."

The day is well under way when we approach the low building that houses the school. Bakiri escorts me to the head mistress. I move to sit next to him and I see her look, which has the same quality that the experienced men have when looking at the war mares brought before them: A quick assessment with intent eyes. She will want to see more, but she already has spotted my gifts for movement.

"Have you had any training?" she asks me, her erect body displaying that she, in her younger days, had been no stranger to the dance.

"No." I reply, raising my chin proudly. I sense that a show of arrogance will impress her more than mere silver or fine linens. Thin, with no softness in expression or body, she measures me with her eyes and her manner. She has survived in a tough world by the force of her will.

Her nostrils flare as she notes that gesture. Her eyes widen as she hears my voice, which I have learned focuses even more attention on me. Her face shows a tinge of what

I have seen on other faces. The war mares evoke the same desire to possess. Her face relaxes slightly, but I see that flash and know what it means. A tightening of Bakiri's eyes alerts me that he, too, has seen the flash.

"Good! You won't have bad habits to overcome. Would you like to see our students as they are taught?"

"Yes," Bakiri and I say at the same time. Serena tried to teach me a surface meekness as a tool to disarm, but I have not perfectly learned and often forget to defer to my elders or anyone else when it is prudent to do so. Speech arrives on my lips before I can consider whether it is wise to utter it. I keep trying to follow Serena's example, but I find it hard and against the trend of my mind.

"Come with me, then. My sons and daughters are the ones who teach the youngsters, just as I taught them."

I follow her as she leads us to where the teaching takes place. My heart will never warm to her, but if the teaching is good, I will be able to learn here.

We go out another door into the courtyard. Buildings surround the central core. A pool of water with bright tiles around the edge is in the center, and I catch the flash of more tiles in the bottom of the pool. It appears as if there are fish swimming in the pool, but then I realize they are tiles made to look like them. The pillars that hold up the roofs are lotus-shaped and painted with bright colors that glow in the hot air. From one building I hear voices raised in song, mixed with the sounds of stringed instruments. I know I must keep my mind on judging what I see before me, instead of doing what I wish to do, which is to break out into song. It is hard to restrain myself.

We go into a large room filled with moving bodies, still bodies, both male and female, of many ages—many colors, too. Some are dark as ebony, others are the warm brown that I am used to. As I look, I can see that there are many groups. Each group works on one gesture, or one dance. My eye is caught by the group that is closest to where we entered. Without thinking anything of it, I move my body and my hands to imitate what I am seeing. The teacher, who has the look of his mother, demonstrates what he wants and the bodies around him try to copy the same gestures. I see it once and I am able to repeat exactly what is being shown.

I hear the gasp behind me. The school mistress gestures to her son, who approaches us. At a quiet word from her, he invites me to join his pupils. With his eyes on me, he makes a more complicated pattern with his feet and his hands. I follow along and reflect them back to him. I respond to his fleeting touch on my elbow, the slight raising of his chin. His grave face softens in pride. I can see that he thinks it is his teaching that is the source of my learning so quickly. The flash that comes into his eyes makes me aware that he is also thinking that teaching me could bring him renown. I wonder if he wishes to possess me to gain a school of his own: A school that would be more famous than his mother's. I keep my face still and show him nothing of my thoughts.

The students around him turn their eyes to me. Some of the eyes are hostile, some are curious, and many more are uninterested. I see by the fine linen that covers their limbs and their finely wrought jewelry that these are the children of the rich. They are used to being deferred to because of their parents' positions, used to having their talents extravagantly praised, whether their talents were marked or not. This is the first time someone other than my kin—or our enemies on the long journey to the Land of the One River—have seen my gifts for the dance. What I see in their eyes is new to me. I keep my face still to cover up the unease that these envious eyes arouse.

One by one, I enter the other circles in the large room. One by one, I test the teachers and they test me. I know who I can work with easily and who I can learn more from, and I also know which hearts and minds are closed to me. I smile at all, even those who can teach me nothing. Serena tried to teach me to disguise myself sufficiently that I did not provoke hatred and envy and make needless enemies. That difficult lesson I imperfectly absorbed.

"I can also show you the other building where the arts of music are taught. It includes both the singing of songs and the playing of instruments."

The head mistress leads us to another large room which opens into the courtyard. It is clear to me that Bakiri is the one whose favor she wishes to cultivate. She flatters him by the tone of her voice. She sizes me up as if I were for sale and she were deciding whether or not to buy. She is making calculations about me that I do not understand, but I am in no doubt that she is only to be trusted to look after her own interests. I sense no passion for the arts she is supposed to be teaching in her school, even though she is trained in some of them.

I look at the stringed instruments with great interest and when one is handed to me, stroke the strings to bring out sounds. I am clumsy but sense I can learn quickly. One teacher leads a group in a song or chant, and although I cannot yet understand all the words, I can follow the music and sing along, almost unaware that I do so.

The teacher's eyes pick me out as I hum along; he cocks his head to hear better and I can see that I please him. I am not surprised, for my songs have pleased many for all of my life. He gives a quick glance to the head mistress, and I can feel, rather than see, her head nod in response. No words have to be used, so no words *are* used.

The headmistress quietly says to Bakiri, "We will be willing to accept Alimah as our student."

Her gleaming eyes show how much she wants me to attend her school, and I can see that my talents, if developed, would add to her prestige. She could then raise her rates and the caliber of her students. Her black eyes show avarice which she cannot conceal. She is intelligent enough to try to acquire my great gifts for her school, but not intelligent enough to realize that I am no mere child to be ordered about. She reaches out to caress me, but before she can touch me, I discreetly remove myself to stand closer to Bakiri. Watching intently, Bakiri gives me a look that I know. I go to his side, showing all that I am under his protection and that he does not welcome others touching me.

He then addresses the head mistress in courteous words. "Thank you so much for the gracious invitation to see your school and pupils. I will inform you of my decision when it has been made. We must be leaving whilst the daylight is still with us."

I follow Bakiri out the door to where our war mares and companions wait. We ride down the dusty trail under the bright clear sky. Crops on either side of us exhale the scents of growing things. In the Land of the One River, clouds are rare, unlike where I spent my younger years. There, clouds would appear, sometimes rain would appear, but every day brought changes. Here, every day is the same for long periods of time. I am not used to it. But, it does not matter for I am here to learn and learn quickly.

Our war mares step daintily. Well trained, they do not start at the birds that swoop, only their pricked ears betray their alert natures. If needed, they would respond quickly, at one with their riders. Their riders, trained in the arts of war, share the alertness of their steeds. While they appear to be casually riding along the trail, their eyes scan the trails and listen to the sounds of birds, alert to any change that might mean danger.

I am excited at the thought of learning more dance and songs and music—still, my heart lurches at the thought of being separated from Bakiri. Like his distant relation Petros the Wise, he is one who can be relied upon.

He looks down at me and says, "We will talk of this later, you and I and our host. This family has not the habits that I have learned from Petros the Wise and all who accompanied him here. They pretend that only one person makes the decisions, even when that is not the case. You and I can talk freely, but you and I will have to be careful with our host."

Later that day, as we stand watching the war mares, we talk.

"What think you of the quality of the instruction?" Bakiri asks.

"I could learn much, but it will not be long before I learned all they can teach me," I reply.

"How long?" He looks interested in my answer.

"The silver moon is now so slight that nothing can be seen when the sun has gone to its daily demise. When that moon becomes so bright that I can see everything that is not in deepest shadow, I will have learned everything that I can."

He looks surprised for a moment and then looks at the war mares, muttering to himself so I can barely hear the words. "It is the same with the war mares: some learn instantly, with others much patience is needed."

He asks in his clear voice, "Do you think I should permit you to enroll there?"

I pause. Then, in a burst of words, "Yes! I think so. But, Uncle Bakiri, I think you should insist that you should collect me every ten risings of the sun and bring me back with you for several days, before returning me to them."

"Why?" Bakiri's brown eyes study me. He is trying to learn how to judge my answers, and to know whether he can trust them. He learns from me as I learn from him how to speak carefully and not just utter words as they occur to me.

"The silver and linen you pay them will be very welcome. My gifts will be very welcome. But I sense something and am not sure what it is, except that I think it would be dangerous to be there unprotected for more than a few risings of the sun. I sense greed in the headmistress and hostility behind the eyes of some of the students, an anger that I understand not. There is something unhealthy in the school that I understand not."

"I, too, sensed something amiss, and could not tell what it was," Bakiri replies. "Should we search further for another school? Will it be too dangerous for you there?"

"I don't know. I need the training, but I sense danger." Hoping that Bakiri, unused to the gifted ones, will understand, I add "Until I came to the Land of the One River I was protected as the gifted ones are protected. Serena taught me much, but still I was protected. I am new to the ways of this world and those who inhabit it."

Bakiri stops and thinks and then says, "You will not reside at the school. I will appoint someone to escort you to the school, stay there during the day, and then escort you back here. With all the danger that has come with the Great Destruction it will not provoke any comment. No one ventures out without being armed and ready for whatever might arise. I will stay here, too. We are old friends, our host and I. We have much in common besides the war mares." He pauses, then says, "I will not conceal from you how deeply uneasy I am at something in the school."

"Did you sense it when we were talking to the head mistress?" I, too, wish to know the source of my uneasiness. I barely notice that he is talking to me not as a female or a child but as someone whose thoughts are worthy.

"No, did you?" His face is grave.

I think carefully. "No. It was only in the room with the teachers and the pupils. But I don't trust the head mistress. She is not one of the gifted ones even if she has been trained in the arts of dance and music. She wants to use my talents for her own ends, which are not mine."

Distaste shows on his face. "I agree with you about her. She is a deceitful woman." He inquires softly, "Was it one of the teachers who made you uneasy? Or was it one or more of the other pupils?"

"The teachers were eager to teach me. Some I can learn from and some I cannot. Those whom I can not learn from will not favor me." I pause, thinking how to give voice to my doubts. "I think, Bakiri, it was one or more of the pupils. It felt as if someone whom I had never seen before took one look and instantly harbored a great hate for me, which does not make sense."

Bakiri looks sadly at me. "Great hatred instantly come upon often does not make sense."

Suddenly, I am almost in tears. I am here in a strange land, far from those I grew up with, far from those I know and understand. Have I taken on too much? Has my thirst to develop my gifts led me to make a big mistake? Perhaps I should have returned with Kaliq and lived life with him, raised children with him.

Sense, and the reality of the life that Kaliq is destined to live, return to me. Kaliq is fated to be one of the leaders of our people and as such he will travel as a protector and travel as one who trades goods. Serena has a traveling mate and I have seen how, at times, she has been alone too much. Even the children that she shares with Lukenow do not completely satisfy her. She has her songs that ease those lonely times. I have seen, though, the looks she and The Bedouin share, especially since their rescue. If Lukenow had not come to reclaim his mate, I wonder what would have happened. I wonder what did happen when The Bedouin and Serena were kept captive in a small room. I know of the ways of men and women when they join their bodies. I know of the looks they wear when they are attracted to each other. Kaliq has that look when he looks at me. I know it, but cannot respond yet. Yet? Ever?

I need the training in the dances and songs and instruments that the Land of the One River has, so I can carry them back as a gift to my people and to Kaliq. I know without any words that I must pursue this training. From the stories of my people, I know that Hoval, the son of Thutmose, was sent into the Land of the One River to train in the arts of working gold and gems. Sardow was lucky, for the one who helped her with her gifts was living near when she needed him. It is my fate that I have had to search out the training. But, like Hoval and Sardow, I will be protected.

At least one set of eyes amongst the pupils seems to seethe at the sight of me. I think those eyes are the source of my unease, and of Bakiri's unease. I tell him of this, but I can tell him no more because I know no more.

It is decided. Tomorrow I will join the classes, and as the sun goes to its daily death in the west, I will return to this safe house, this haven.

Chapter Five

The School of the Arts of Music and Dance

Pupils bringing silver or linen to pay for lessons were always accepted. Terms were agreed on: I was welcomed the next morning. Most of the students live in the surrounding buildings. I will not, and know it will set me apart from the other students—more apart than even my talents and my coming from afar will.

Bakiri says his farewells and makes it clear that he will return for me as the sun makes its way to its nightly demise. He leaves several young men at the school as guards. It does not appear unusual and excites no comment.

Menes, one of Bakiri's many sons, is included in my group of protectors. He has learned the warrior trades during the wars with the Evil One. Menes has chosen the young woman to be his mate but they do not yet live together. In public he treats me as an honored guest, but in private he treats me as he does his sisters. He teases me, pretends to bully me, and struts his male stuff before me. I have seen him in the midst of chaos and killing where he was calm, focused and effective. Those tumultuous times have left him with a taste for adventure. I know Bakiri is concerned, for Menes is whom Bakiri hopes will take his place in the care of the war mares. Bakiri has learned, however slowly and unwillingly, to bend to the desires of the young. Menes is destined to be one of the protectors.

Fahim, a son from the house of our host, will be a great asset for he knows all the locals and knows with whom to talk to gather bits of gossip and rumors that will help protect us. He looks just like his father. He observes how Menes treats me, and treats me in just the same way. Perhaps because I am small, these vigorous young men see me as a younger sister to be protected and teased.

The last of the group, but not least, is Kadem, a young warrior who has traveled with us from our far away land along the great trade route. Kadem has been tested in many wars, which makes him different from the others who will guard me. That difference shows in the scars that decorate him: mementos of the many skirmishes he has survived. I know him well. He does not joke with me—or from what I can tell, with anyone. His eyes do not rest on me as a man's eyes rest on a woman, but are always alert to everyone around him. He is here to not only teach the ways of war to those who would learn from him, but also to learn of the Land of the One River, to understand it and to make contacts here that will be useful when those of our kin come again to this dangerous place.

He has taught the other protectors how to use the silver bow and swift arrows to defeat those who would overwhelm us with brute force. All his troop of protectors have readily equipped themselves with the new weapon, and have achieved mastery over the arrows that can defeat their enemies. Kadem knows who made the powerful bows and has seen to it that the other young men are well-equipped.

I know that the protectors always look for weapons that will give them more of an advantage over any who mean us harm. I have become so used to it that I no longer pay any attention, although I notice that each new weapon could cause more harm. As we made our way down the Great Green Sea to the Land of the One River, we saw more and more of the Great Destruction. Sometimes it was hard to see that loveliness still existed, surrounded as we were by danger and evil. Serena's wise words steadied me as I looked upon hard sights. She had taught me well.

From the looks the students give my protectors, I think that they will not be lonely. Shining in the sun, young and robust, they lounge at their ease near their war mares. I know they will not be so distracted that they will forget their guard duties. Their alert eyes promise that. One or more of them is always on patrol. Their seeming ease is just that: seeming. One of our host's youngsters gives me a glance and struggles to keep his mouth that was made for laughter firm. I hope he will never lose that laughter. I remember I had sung and danced at Bakiri's home, once the scary times were behind us. The young men had to do hard things in cleansing the Evil One's compound. They saw hard things. I thought to distract them from the ugliness with my songs and dances. I did. I saw their faces soften, the hard lines erased by pleasure as, for a short time, they could forget the killing and disease.

"Thank you, Alimah. You have lightened our hearts with your songs." So said Menes at that time.

It is time to step forward out of the past. I am ready to learn. I am thirsty to learn.

All the pupils walk through the courtyard. I and they pass the fragrant plants and the pools filled with water, a place to be out of the hot brightness of the day. We stride past the brightly-painted columns shaped like lotus leaves that hold up the doors, and that provide a grace and color to the sandy earth.

I see a beam of the life-giving sun shine on the waving hair of one student. His hair glitters in the sun like the gold it so reminds me of. I glance again: his eyes are the color of the sky, although shaded by dark lashes. Taller than the other students, his muscled body gleams softly as he proudly walks to his class. No one walks by his side, or close to him. I have heard of such creatures who come from a far away land, but I have never seen one. He holds himself with the quiet confidence of one who commands.

His eyes meet mine, for I have paused, dazzled by the sight of him. I wonder instantly if he is the cause of the hostility I have sensed in some of the others, here to learn the traditional arts. I sense no hostility in him. I see, though, that the others regard him warily, as if he were a dangerous exotic animal loosed amongst them. I catch a flash of something in his eyes, and do not know what it means, just that it is not an unwholesome lust or hostility.

I join the group of the teacher from the day before. We practice. I have become fluent in the tongue of those who live in the Land of the One River. As I perfect the

29

movements that the teacher shows us, I am able to see which of my fellow dancers resent me and which do not. Low muttered phrases, said too quickly for me to understand, are followed by stifled laughter that I know is aimed at me. One of the less talented girls comes close to me and bumps into me as I am executing a move. I know it is deliberate for she is not that clumsy. I could have taken a dangerous fall, if I were careless. She looks at me insolently and says nothing, as if I were a servant not worthy of notice. I stare at her and utter a phrase that one of Bakiri's sons taught me. Her eyes widen as she backs away. The phrase works, maybe too well, for I know I have made an enemy.

Whether this hostility arises from my being from a far land or from my obvious talents for the dance disturbs me not. Neither one can I remedy, and Serena has warned me that no gestures on my part can change those minds which are against me at their first sight.

I am here to learn the arts of dance and of making songs. I senses that I could use the sounds from the strings of the graceful lyres to escort my songs. Birds, when they break into song, meld their sounds with the other sounds of the fertile earth. I wish to add to the songs that crowd their way out of me, to make them more beautiful so that those who hear will remember them always. When I have learned all that I can from this small school, which caters to the rich and untalented, I will leave. What path I should then seek is not clear to me. I have in this one day, seen what there is to be learned of the dance. It will not take long to absorb it. Will it be the same with the music making?

What of the Golden One who catches my eye? What mystery lies there?

Chapter Six

The Golden One Sees Alimah

My people are far away in the frozen north, where the brisk winds from the great sea sweep the cobwebs from our eyes so we can see clearly. The mead hall, filled with song and laughter, is where I come from. The mead hall where the men—my men—boast of their valor and courage, is where I will return. It is not like this land that lies supine under the constant sun. This land smells of long hot days and the growing of crops after the flooding. Not for this land, the crisp air of my home in the far country.

The other students mill about chattering as they wait for their teachers to start their day's exercises. The other students are not only young but lack the wits to live without their rich families. They have never been tested in the world, and think they never will be.

I have seen the roving bands of desperate people fleeing from war and famine. And I know that terrible changes are coming and cannot be avoided. I have seen the villages smoldering in their remains. I have seen the bodies of those slaughtered. I do not think most of these students will survive in hard times. I bring the patience of those who hunt dangerous sea beasts as I wait to return to my people. I will go back to those valiant men who are my family.

Standing by myself as always, for I am alone and distrusted in this strange land, I look around me to see where danger lies so that it does not come upon me unawares. A band of young warriors from the Land of the One River rides into the school. Most of them are garbed in the local style—one with a grim visage comes from far away, his robes more like the ones who live on the Great Desert, a great silver bow slung over his shoulder. Daggers and swords glitter against polished brown skin. All are mounted on the famous war mares whose sleek muscles glow under silver and brown pelts as they prance along on their dainty hooves. The graceful war mares with their watchful riders encircle the precious one whom they protect. They halt and all slide off the backs of their horses. As the dust settles, I see her.

At first she seems but a child, but then I see that no, she is not a child. One leg sweeps over the war mare's back and then she stands on the sandy earth. She seems to not touch the ground as she walks, so light she floats. Her fine linens lie on her as if grateful for the privilege. Her small head above her graceful neck is held erect with all the pride of one born to make beauty: bright eyes, long hair that the slight winds play with. The hand she holds out to one of her guards is as graceful as the big hunting cats. I wait to hear her speak, for such a lovely creature could be spoiled by a coarse voice. Then I hear her and know she is made for joyous songs. Her very speech and laughter are a song, and I know without seeing more of her that she makes beauty with her songs and lithe body.

All the world seems silent as if contemplating her beauty. I stop breathing, for she is a treasure worth more than the other goods that we gather to take back to our cold land— spices and fragrant oils, fine linens, the bright metals that make men go mad, and the bright stones that capture men's fancies. I have never seen such a creature, never dreamed that such a creature could exist. My body stirs. I must have her to take back with me to my own lands. She is well guarded but I must have her. I will take her, just as I take all else that I desire—take her by force, if need be. One day, some time, she will not be so well guarded and then I can seize her and make her mine.

My life and destiny are already set; my mate awaits me at our home. We must have strong sons to keep our people safe. As a leader, I can have many mates, as many as I can gather and protect.

A chill comes over me. How can I have her? Will this lovely creature be able to make the long harsh journey? Some song birds wilt and die if they are captured. Perhaps she is like them and cannot be removed from where she is cherished. Some goods we do not try to bring back to my people, for they are too fragile to survive the journey.

Surprised, I think that only the thought of her perishing will stay my hand, for I cannot be part of destroying such beauty. But still, my body stirs and tells me that I want her for my own. I must have her for my own. I will have her for my own.

Chapter Seven

Alimah and The Golden One Become Friends

I dangle my bare feet in the pool as I eat the bread, dates and the fruit that Bakiri's host provides for my mid-day meal. I feel a presence next to me and turn my head to meet eyes that are reflected in the arching sky above. I had not realized how large he was until this moment when he sits next to me. All about him is gold, except for those startling eyes. Long limbs covered with fine hairs glint gold in the shining light. His wavy hair is a radiance around his head, giving off shards of light. The sun has polished his limbs to a golden color—even his long fingers seem different than those of the others. They are.

Gold is revered in the Land of the One River: used to escort the dead to their next life, used to intimidate and fill with lust rulers from other lands. I wonder why this golden person is not captured and exhibited as a gift from the gods. I know that I have ventured into a tangle of things I do not understand, and know I must be wary and discreet. Bakiri might unravel what is going on, but I sense that he is sometimes as confused as I am. In this moment I long for Kaliq, who is quiet but knowing. He could understand and teach me.

Alas, Kaliq is not here, so I will have to sharpen my own wits and figure it out myself.

"They do not want to share my food or my presence. Some think I am one of the sea peoples who cause such troubles here and elsewhere. Others think I am a mere barbarian. What do you think?" His voice is deep, his accent slight.

"It seems they think the same of me. I will share what I have with you. I do not sense that you are a danger to me."

The Golden One settles himself next to me and dangles his feet in the pool as I do. "I will share what I have with you. I sense that *you* are not a danger to *me*," he says gravely. My first thought is that he is teasing me. But no, I see no signs of teasing. I will not be as a younger sister to him.

I peel a piece of fruit and give him half. It is sweet and welcome to both of us. We rinse our fingers in the pond, and rinse the sweet juices off our chins—then we smile at each other.

He speaks in the slow cadence of one who uses a language new to him. "You seem not from the Land of the One River, but you know how they speak and the one who brought you here is from this land. That is a mystery, but what is not a mystery are your gifts. They leap out from your very first gesture."

"I am here to learn the arts of the dance, and of the music and songs as they are taught in the Land of the One

River. When I have absorbed what there is to be absorbed here, I may go elsewhere to learn more. I have no time to waste." I know not why I add that last statement. Maybe I want nothing to do with a person who is not serious.

"I, too, have no time to waste." His voice, not quite fluent in the local habits of speech, nevertheless is very clear. He seems as focused as I on learning as much as he can in a short period of time. I wonder if he is a gifted one from another land.

"Why?" I ask.

"My people need me to learn certain things and then return to them." One muscle quivers in his serious face.

"You are destined to be your people's leader." I speak before I think it through carefully. Serena has tried to teach me to think before speaking, but it is hard for me to remember.

He looks startled and then suspicious. "Why do you say that? How could you possibly know that?"

Regretting my having disturbed him with my words, my reply is calm: "You remind me of the leader of my own people and you remind me of the one who will be the next leader." I spare a thought for Petros the Wise and Kaliq, whose inner certainty is so much like this Golden One. Maybe I should have gone back with Kaliq as he desired. In a flash, I remember Kaliq rescuing me from those who would capture me, and how he put me in front of him on his swift war mare and rode away from danger. His warm arms encircled me—he warmed my back, my legs, all of me. I felt his every muscle. I get a small thrill as I recall it.

"It is not the man who brought you here, or the ones who stay all day to guard you?" He still looks disturbed, but not so dismayed.

"No." I do not want to disclose more. I remember that voices carry very well here and I do not know him well. All I know are his looks, and that the other pupils want nothing to do with him. That is not enough to make him safe to confide in.

He looks at me. "I have learned much here. I will use it to protect my people." He holds his head proudly, his hair shining gold—so different from those others among us.

"I will learn much, too." Then a new thought comes to me, one obvious when I utter it. "My people also need my skills." My lips curve in a not-to-be-hidden smile. I have learned much from this stranger.

He gives me a startled look. "Shall we share our food again?" He is asking more, of course. Shall we talk, begin a friendship?

I reply, "Yes." I pause and add, "I will like that."

I wonder what his skin will feel like under my fingertips. I have never wondered that about Kaliq.

Chapter Eight

Alimah Tells Bakiri of the Golden-Haired Stranger

Bakiri asks of me, "Your guards told me of you sharing some sweet fruit with the golden-haired stranger. Who is he?"

My protectors tell Bakiri and the elders all of what they see at the school. That is their job. I answer calmly. "The others who are there to learn will not speak with him or keep him company either because they think he is one of the Sea Peoples or because they think he is a barbarian."

"Is he one of the Sea Peoples?" Bakiri inquires with raised eyebrows.

I shrug my shoulders. "Not that I know of or that he admits. He says he is here to learn and then go back and lead his people." I am hungry but must wait until this conversation is completed.

"Did he say who his people are?" Bakiri looks uneasy.

"No," I answer. "I did not ask him. I did not think it right. This was the first time we spoke together."

"Do you think he is the source of our unease about this school?" This question is uppermost in Bakiri's mind, as it should be.

"No, I don't think so. I could be wrong, but I don't think so. When I left the pond and our lunch and went back to the classes, I was again aware of a hidden hostility." I am quite sure of this, for I sense the hatred as I learn the new ways of dance and song.

"Was it one of the students or one of the teachers who is the source of the hostility?" Bakiri is relentless. As leader of his people he cannot be careless. I am more and more reminded of Petros the Wise, who when asking questions will not stop until he has answers that satisfy him.

"I am not sure, but I think it is more than one person. They do not suspect that I am one of the Sea Peoples but they know I come not from their land. The other students make me feel unwelcome as a stranger and a barbarian. I have never encountered this before. I have found hostility because of the kin I come from, but this is something different. Harsher."

I had a sudden thought. "Perhaps it is not me? Could it be something here that provokes the hostility? Some enemy of yours, perhaps?"

"Good thinking. I already asked your protectors of their thoughts. They picked up on the hostility, too, and noticed that it increased the closer they came to you. I asked if any of them recognized any of the students, and they said no." Bakiri is puzzled.

I search for an answer. "But would a younger child of your enemies be recognized amongst so many other youngsters?"

"It is doubtful. I wonder, Alimah, if you have stumbled into a blood feud in that school. You know how they fester for generations and then break out again." His face saddens at the memory of the Evil One who had to be destroyed. "I am growing more and more certain, although I don't have more than suspicion to be certain about."

"How should I act then? Ignore it? Be wary? Learn as much as I can of the dance in as short a period as I can so I can leave?" I need this answer to know how to protect myself.

"That sounds right to me, Alimah. We may have to cut short your stay there, and our stay here. I have a feeling it will get more dangerous." Bakiri now looks worried.

"What of my new friend, the Golden One?" I ask.

Bakiri replies, "Surely he has his own people who look out for him?"

"I don't know." I realize that I, too, am uneasy.

Bakiri looks at me keenly, wondering if there is more to this than friendship. Wondering if because I am young, that I do not know my mind about who will be my mate. No sense in telling him I know what I am doing. I have noticed that the Protectors tend to disregard the thoughts of the young, especially if they are female. One thinks they would have learned from Sardow, Salama, Serena, and my revered ancestor Hasna to not have such unworthy thoughts. The Protectors are born to protect and can not and will not stop, any more than they can stop breathing the sweet air.

40

Chapter Nine

Alimah Learns While the Moon Grows Larger

I must learn quickly. The hostility that I sense seems more intense the longer I remain at the school. In the dance I study with the few who have something of worth to teach me. The teachers who do not, I do not bother with. They resent it, for they can see my gifts, but I trust not their teaching. I know that nothing I do or say will change how they think of me.

In the room with the music instruments, I do the same, and I become friends with the makers of the instruments. I can tell that some of the younger ones can be persuaded to make instruments for others. They are not always treated well by their teachers and I can tell by the looks in their eyes that, like myself, they are learning all they can as swiftly as possible.

Those who teach song teach me little, for I know more than they. A few of the teachers help me with little things.

Most tend to throw up their hands and not even try. Always, my gift for song has been strongly marked, and few could teach me anything. I learn a few tricks of how to hold my breath and my audience's attention. How to focus attention where I wish it to be focused. These things the teachers bring to me, but little else.

When the sun reaches its height and I have learned all I can, I go alone to relax by the pool and wait for The Golden One to join me. I know by now that, although he has gifts in the dance and the song, that he is not driven as I am. He applies himself and every day looks more wary. It seems as if the only place either of us can cease being wary is by the pool.

"How did it go today, Alimah?" he asks, and listens to my answer.

I tell him and then ask the same question of him. We share fruit, share the sweet juices that run down our chins, share what there is of food to sustain us. We both notice the gritty nature of the bread that is caused by the encroaching and ever-present sand. Sometimes I bring things for him to eat, but not often enough so that he might feel obligated. His manners, wherever he has learned them, are perfect. We talk using the words that are used in the Land of the One River. To speak in another language that we both know would, we sense, bring even more troubles down on us.

We speak of the hostility that we both notice is directed at both of us for reasons neither of us can understand. We slowly empty our minds to each other, cautious at first, but eventually learning to trust one another. I tell him some stories of my kin. He tells me nothing of his. I suppress my anger as I sense other reasons for his not telling me. What they are I cannot imagine. But we are open about which of the students are sources of hostility towards each of us. We acquit the teachers but cannot decide which of the pupils is the source. Since none of the other students will talk freely to either one of us, we can learn no more. So we have to be content, and I try to be more discreet, to not say what has just entered my mind.

He looks at me and sometimes there is a glint in his eye. He carefully does not touch me, ever. I look at his long fingers and wonder what they would feel like on my skin. I wish to touch him, but do not. Perhaps it shows in my eyes. We carefully never touch each other, but talk and talk until someone comes and reminds us to go to our classes.

The Golden One walks me to my protectors after classes are over for the day. He runs his fingers over the muzzle of my war mare, then over her sleek neck. I find that I am jealous of her, that I want his fingers on me, not her. He greets my protectors every day, and then waits as I slide onto the war mare and ride away. His golden hair gleams in the afternoon sun and heat as we ride away, leaving him behind, a solitary figure surrounded by those who know him not and wish him ill.

My protectors notice but say nothing. No teasing, no questions, but they notice.

Since the day when we saw a destroyed chariot and a war mare with its legs chopped off, Bakiri and our host have added even more well-armed young men to our protective troop. Rumors have reached us of new swords that are as tall as a man and can cleave a man in half or destroy a chariot or a war mare. While at the school waiting for me to finish, my protectors are more on guard than ever. Their eyes never cease probing for the sight of those who mean harm. Even the students who take their safety and high status as birth rights look uneasy. I think most of them have not the wits to survive whatever is coming. Even though they have not welcomed me, I find I can have pity for them in their ignorance of what lies ahead of them.

Our host and Bakiri plot how to protect those under their care, the people and the war mares. They have to protect their land from the coming destruction.

Chapter Ten

The Golden One Considers Alimah

I have learned her name and something of her. I have seen her in the classrooms and seen how the teachers recognize her great talents. The other students want nothing to do with her, which is a puzzle to me.

Alimah carefully explains to me that it has been thus with her since she began this great journey. She tells me of how she has learned not to care or to try to make friends, for her great gifts set her apart. She tells me of how Serena, who is of her kin and has the gift for songs, has taught her to read the hearts of those not of the kin and so, to protect herself.

I see that her spirits have not been crushed, for her people know how to cherish the gifted ones. She tells me this and I see the care that her guards take with her. They do not want her like I want her. They treat her as they might a younger sister: guard her, tease her and leave her strictly alone in the way of a man with a woman.

How can they ignore her great beauty that makes her gifts shine? Perhaps, they know she is not made for a domestic life. Perhaps they think she would not be a comfortable mate and mother to their children. Perhaps she has already been claimed by one of their leaders. That seems more likely to me, for she could only be the mate of a man who leads other men and can protect her.

The more I speak with her and the more time I spend with her the more I want to be with her, listen to her, play with her. When I hear her voice raised in song, I stop and can only listen, for the song that pours out of her makes my heart stop. Others around me are also quieted.

She comes on silent feet to sit beside me at the pool; I know she is there by the fresh scent that comes with her and announces her presence. Her fine linens drape her body and move as she moves. She dangles her feet in the water. Even her toes are graceful.

Among my people the women are valued for the fine sons they bring into being. If barren they are still cared for, but only the mothers of fine sons are revered. The men of my family do not become too attached to any one woman, for that attachment would interfere with the manly pursuits of war and trade. It would be unseemly and dangerous.

I must have her. I must make her my own. But I cannot. The more I know of her, the more I want her. The more I see of her, the more I know I must be careful. I must not bring harm to this glorious creature.

Chapter Eleven

Alimah Learns from the Bull Dancers

Because I am so small, as they are, the dancers from the far away island are eager to practice with me. Perhaps they are lonely, being in a strange land. Perhaps they are bored and want to teach me. The dancers who are here have escaped the Great Destruction that has touched their land. I learn to bend my body in the lithe way of these dancers, and want to fly through the air from a toss, want to use the others bodies to fly through the air.

This form of the dance requires that I trust the hands and bodies of my partners, for one wrong toss could lead to disaster and injuries that would never heal. I see that a clumsy or inattentive partner can lead to a crumpled figure on the ground who will never move again.

I sense that, even here with these dancers, the hostility lives. During the long day, and under the eyes of the teachers, I learn all that I can learn, and accustom my body to what are strange movements. I learn all of these either with my feet on the dusty ground or, as I know more, using my weight and muscles to spring through the air, practicing again and again until I perfect the moves.

Something about the others makes me reluctant to be partners in their more daring moves. A flash of eyes, a muttered curse. I trust them not.

The Golden One says to me late one afternoon, as the glowing sun was making its way to its daily death, "I see that you are learning the moves of the Bull Dancers."

"The Bull Dancers?" I reply, for I am only vaguely aware of what Bull Dancers refers to.

He explains to me. "On their native island, these dancers would be in an arena with bulls. They would toss each other above the bulls' horns, avoiding death and injury. When the bulls rushed them they would seize the horns and use that force to lift themselves high in the air, unharmed."

"How did you come to have this knowledge? I thought their land had been caught in the Great Destruction." I want to learn more.

"Their feats are renowned among my people. One of their dancers took refuge with my people and taught us curious youngsters something of his art." He takes a deep breath and continues, almost shyly, "I notice you do not yet let the others toss you into the air. Is there a reason?"

"Something in me says their hands are not safe," I say with a rush.

He studies me, and then his face hardens. "Would you trust my hands to catch you?"

"Yes." I say this without thinking, knowing that I want to master the flying moves but only with a trusted partner.

His face softens. Surely he knows by now that I trust him. "We have some time before you must leave with your escort. Come and I will show you how."

And so he teaches me the rest of the Bull Dancers' moves. He puts out his hand, I put one foot in its warm steadiness and then spring to stand on his broad shoulders. I balance quickly. He then walks slowly as again I balance surely. He pivots and still I hold my balance. He quickly kneels in the dust, spreading his hands wide as I flip over his head and land firmly on the ground. No falls, no quivering from either of us. His steady strength is the base on which I perfect the Bull Dancers' moves.

Soon we attract an audience. The teachers look with sharp eyes and notice all the moves we make. The Bull Dancers, tiny and strong, look at the Golden One with startled eyes, wondering no doubt where he has learned such moves. I sense flashes of hostility but as usual cannot identify from whom they emanate.

We become the center of attention. It is as if the Golden One could not resist working with me, but also as if in working with me he bares a secret that is important enough to have been hidden.

The more we practice the easier it becomes. We grow accustomed to each other's bodies, my small hand in his large one. I know when he is about to make a move that will catapult me through the air. I know that when I return to earth I will be safe in his hands or else land so that I am safe on my feet. These moments of flying through the air are exhilarating; I wish to fly higher and longer. I practice sleeking out my body, stretching my arms into the cloudless sky, pointing my feet to leave the earth behind, making a cooling wind with my passage into the air.

At night, as I sleep, I often dream of flying, flying into the hot air, and then flying up into the night air, flying close to the stars and touching them with my outstretched fingers. I am captivated.

"Have you tried standing on your war mare's back?" The Golden One asks.

I am learning about him. "No, I never thought of doing that. Did you learn that in your far away land?"

"Yes." His face closes down again.

"What use is it, or is it for beauty and the entertainment of others?" My eyes must have lit up, for he smiled down at me.

"No, it is a technique of fighting that has use in some dire circumstances," he says. "Arrows can be used by those trained in this art. Some can leap from war mare to war mare, which disconcerts those they are fighting."

"Can you do this?"

He smiles at me again, his eyes warming. "What do you think?"

"I think yes, or else you would not have told me of it. It seems you only tell me things that you are already a master of." I am certain of this.

"You want to learn, don't you?"

What a silly question! Of course I want to learn. Why does he ask? He already knows the answer.

"Yes. Will you teach me?"

So he teaches me. We practice at the end of the day. We practice when we sit by the pool and eat our few scraps of food. I arrive at the school earlier and earlier so that we have even more time to practice.

As our bodies become more and more harmonious, our minds know each other. It is like Kaliq and Dalil who,

50

having grown up with each other, need not language to know the other's thoughts and reactions. At the thought of Kaliq I pause. I have not thought of him for such a long time. He has faded from my thoughts where he used to occupy much of them. But now, I am learning, absorbing so much that is new and exciting, that I have no thought to spare for him who will, someday, be my mate.

I know not exactly what I have to learn in the Land of the One River, have only a vague but deep desire to learn more of the dance and song than I already know. But here I am, learning something I knew not existed, learning how to perform these works for an audience. I learn how to hold the audience's attention, how to make the people in the audience lose touch with what is going on around them.

I notice from my perch above the Golden One's head that those who watch us are so attentive that they notice not a feral dog that wanders among them, or that they brush away a goat that butts against them. The Evil One, lately vanquished, used the red seeds from the Land of the Bull Dancers to confuse their minds. This way could be much better.

It comes to me when flying through the air that these entertainments could be used to conceal other purposes—that while everyone is looking only at the Golden One and me, something else could be taking place. I wonder how this could be useful to the kin. I tuck the thought away as if it were a precious glowing jewel, not useful at the moment, but to be taken out when the time is right, and brought to life.

Chapter Twelve

The Golden One Is Surprised by Alimah

As we practice the arts of the Bull Dancers, I begin to understand that there is more to Alimah than even I thought. She catches on quickly to what I can teach her. When she puts her small foot trustingly in my hand to vault to my shoulders and with perfect balance stands, I realize the strength in that delicate body.

She has a far away look on her face and then looks at me with glowing eyes. "I can use the force of another to protect myself, just like the Bull Dancers use the rush of the maddened bull to speed their way into flight," she says.

I look my question.

"I say it clumsily. If someone were to rush at me with ill intent, instead of trying to fight which I have not the strength to do, what if I use the strength of their headlong rush to evade them?"

She shakes her head in frustration. "I have not the words. Here, let's try it."

I make a mock rush at her; she melts away and I find my rush has ended in nothing but confusion. She cleverly uses my superior strength to disarm me, and then she emerges whole and triumphant.

We try again, and she gains in precision even though she has not the words to describe what she is doing.

"Alimah!" I gasp. "You are a wonder! This will work. Perhaps it will even work against daggers. We need to practice."

The feel of her hands in mine, the feel of tossing her into the air as if she were a bird taking flight, the brush of her limbs against mine, the sound of her laughter, all these will be with me forever. I want more, my body wants more. I dream of her at night. I dream of being inside her. I wake up aching with my need.

Every sound, every scent, every glimpse of her increases my desire for her. I can easily overpower Alimah and make her mine. It would be easy, for she already trusts me and wants me as a woman wants a man. But how I could I keep her safe during the long harsh journey to my home? And then what? In the cold lands she, to whom I owe my duty and who is already my mate, awaits me. We need to have strong sons to lead and protect our people. What then, of Alimah? I wish my wise uncle were here to tell me more of the ways of the women of the kin. He has traveled widely and knows much. I need his wisdom. In my mind, I circle back to when first I saw her and realize, yet again, that I can do nothing to harm this glorious creature.

Chapter Thirteen

Menace

At the end of the crowded day it is a relief to return to my familiar war mare and to those who guard me. The Golden One, as usual, walks with me to my protectors. I pat the soft muzzle of my war mare and feed her a treat I have saved from my own food. I smile at my protectors, say a reluctant goodbye to The Golden One and off we ride away from the school.

"What did you learn from those who came to talk with you?" I ask, partly in mischief and partly in curiosity. We ware well on the way to where we all are staying. I am comfortable with my protectors. By this time we know each other well. They also know that when hard times come, I can be relied upon, for the two protectors who have known me longer have told our host's son of our adventures and my part in them.

Menes says with a knowing smile: "The girl students, as usual, came and cooed over the war mares and tried out their dances and songs on us. They looked at us from under their eye lashes and sinuously walked where we could see them. The boy students, as is usual with young men, came and watched the war mares with great shining eyes, wanting to ask if they could ride, and prevented by the courtesies they must practice from asking. But we could see what they wanted. We could also see what the girls wanted. Our fine linens and war mares attracted the girls' attentions. Our fine linens and war mares attracted the boys attentions, but for different reasons." My protectors smile down on me, enjoying my sharing their laughter.

Their mouths tighten and I am reminded again that they are all here to protect me.

The one who has known me the longest, my kinsman Kadem, says: "Alimah, I don't wish to alarm you, but I sensed something in one of the students and I don't know which one, or ones. It may be only one or it may be more than one. Something I do not understand but do not trust and do not like. I have told the elders about it. Be careful, Alimah, be careful."

I reply thoughtfully: "In a way I am glad that you sense it, for both Bakiri and I and my new friend, The Golden One, sensed the same. It is why I will not sleep there and why you are sent as my protectors. It disturbs me. I am learning quickly so I can leave the school with no regrets. If I could never return after today and I would have learned enough to satisfy me."

"You have no idea who or why?" Menes, Bakiri's son, asks me.

Calmly I reply to his question: "No. It is beyond what I have found ordinary. Some do not like me because of my gifts. I never encountered it before but am becoming used to it. Serena taught me well. But this is different."

My protectors give me strange looks. "You speak very calmly of those who dislike you because of your gifts.

My sisters would never speak this way of those who like them not."

In a quiet voice I reply, "I do not like it but there is nothing I can do. I have accepted that there are those who are my enemies, not for anything I have done, but for what and who I am."

Suddenly alert, Fahim, the son of our host, puts out his hand out, signaling us to follow. Swiftly and silently we take off across the field to the tall grasses, the tall grasses that promise concealment. We pause as he puts his fingers to his mouth in a shushing motion. From the tension in his shoulders we already know that we must be still. The war mares stand absolutely quiet—not even their proud tails move. I feel the bunched muscles under my legs, ready for instant action if needed.

We hear two riders go by, the jangling noise seemingly made by daggers and swords. We hear their quiet talk, but being in the tall grasses we cannot make out all of what they are saying.

Then we hear one say, "I know not where they have hidden themselves. I did not think any were aware that we were tracking them. Those whom we serve will not be pleased that we have lost them." Then they mutter something we cannot hear, but I hear the words, "The Golden One" clearly. The one who speaks sounds rough and brutal.

Fahim puts his fingers to his lips again as he nods at me. He also, has heard. His face hardens so the genial big brother that I have become accustomed to changes into a warrior, bent on protecting all those in his charge.

We follow Fahim, or rather our war mares follow in his trail. We silently ride through the tall grasses. All are quiet. We come out on a dusty trail that I recognize not, but Fahim, who has grown up here, knows where to go. We follow him and then come to another even smaller trail, until we reach our host's house suddenly from a direction that is new to us.

Bakiri stands by the fences containing the war mares. I see that he is ready to leave. I also see the tension in his shoulders, and wonder at it. Something has disturbed him. When he sees us his face relaxes in relief. He signals to his host and comes up to us.

Bakiri queries Fahim, Menes and Kadem, my daytime protectors, "What happened? I see that something did. I worried when you did not return at your usual time."

Fahim reports to Bakiri and his father: "We have seen these men, and those like them before. One had a scar that reached across his nose, distorting his face. It took just the once—I will never forget his face, and not just because of the scar. He is brutal and fearless. They were not on war mares but made a lot of noise as they rode along. They were heavily armed with daggers and the long swords we have heard of."

Fahim continues speaking. "They were tracking us. We evaded them because I know trails that they did not, because I am from here and they are not. They may be hired, or they may be on their own. They mean us ill."

Bakiri looks at me as I stand quietly by my war mare, my arm over her neck. I am shaken by my protectors' grim faces. He speaks to me.

"This is dangerous. You shall not return to the school. Something is very wrong. We can find you another school."

"I have learned much even in the short time I have spent there. The moon is at the full and I do not need to learn more as I have learned all that I can. Even if I had not, I agree that it would be dangerous to return."

It seems that I can completely relax now. Somehow, though, I know that the story of whomever wishes me harm is not done. Something has been set in motion that has yet to be finished. My thoughts that I do not give voice to return to The Golden One.

Chapter Fourteen

The Golden One Is Injured

I waken suddenly without knowing why my heart pounds. Below me I hear the rapid tramp of feet, the metallic sounds of weapons. Then I hear distant shouts, and the beat of horses' hooves comes closer and closer. I hastily put on my day robes, seize my dagger and go to the window.

The moonlight quivers—a horse carrying a slumped burden enters the courtyard. The figure slides off, then tries to stand and walk, but can only stand swaying in the bright moonlight, leaning on the horse that has brought him here. The horse stands with its head down, gasping for breath. The man, too, is gasping for breath.

Moonlight glints on a dagger that his pursuer swoops in to use. Other men bent on murder come with him. The courtyard is suddenly filled with large armed men who seem possessed by fury. There is fighting in the courtyard; it is hard to see what is happening because the dust rises and curls around the sweating bodies of the men who fight to defend our compound and those who invade to bring murder and desolation. I see Kadem in the midst of the turmoil, his face set and his dagger and sword slashing, felling those who lack the sense to retreat.

Fahim seizes the hand that holds a dagger aimed to make a fatal thrust into the injured one. I hear Fahim yelling, and then I hear the crack of a breaking arm. The dagger falls to the ground. Before he, who was bent on murder, can be captured and questioned, one of his own companions quickly slits his throat. Fahim balks of his prey, tries to capture this new enemy, but he eludes Fahim's grasp and melts into the band of attackers. More of our men and our host's men swarm into the courtyard. Outnumbered, the attackers ride off, slitting the throats of all the injured ones who cannot escape with them. The noise abates.

The clear air, so recently filled with the murderous curses and clashes of daggers and swords and the tumultuous sounds of horses' hooves is now quiet. Quiet returns as we stare, stunned at the still forms on the ground. They lay there and I know they will answer no questions for they have gone to be with their ancestors. What is so important that these men are killed before they can be made to tell what they know? What is so important that all the injured are killed so they cannot reveal secrets?

The Golden One, for it is he who stands swaying beside the exhausted horse, is instantly surrounded and helped to the torch-lit gardens. Dark splotches of blood disfigure his smooth skin. He is laid upon a bench, where his dangling hand drips more blood. His? Or someone else's? His chest heaves as if he has run a long distance. Injuries have depleted his energy.

All are quiet as he is tended to. I can hardly breathe. Have I caused this? Then I realize that I have been in as much danger as he.

"Is he badly hurt?" I ask, trying to remain calm.

Our host replies to me, "The healer says no. Bruises and a few shallow cuts. Nothing broken, but he was badly beaten."

"Who did this to you?" Kadem asks of him.

The Golden One responds, still sounding short of breath.

"There are those who are the enemy of your gifted one, as well as myself. I do not know why. They came for me tonight, meaning great harm. They came with knives and cudgels. I escaped them. I, too, know how to use a dagger and other weapons."

He pauses for breath and then continues, his words slurring with the pain that he cannot escape. "I took their fleetest horse to warn you before they descended upon you. I could tell they were experienced in killing and fighting."

He pauses for he had only enough breath to talk slowly and with many pauses. "They also said they knew how to loosen the tongues of those they held captive. I doubted them not."

The healer keeps working as he speaks, cleaning his wounds and making sure no bones have been broken. The healer then holds a cup to his lips after raising his head, to give our guest a restoring drink. He gasps as he swallows, but then is able to speak with more clarity. He moves without so much pain, too.

His voice becomes stronger. "Someone in that school knows something and summoned these evil ones. It will be more dangerous because of what I heard and also because I injured them and escaped. They will be seeking their revenge."

61

Our host asks of him, "What did you hear that brought you to us?"

"My attackers said that they would take care of the gifted one next. That they would come here to capture her. I came to warn you."

Bakiri has a look on his face that is much like the look that Petros the Wise has when having to make plans quickly: an intent look that signals that he is thinking quickly and deciding whom to trust. The other young warriors become, if anything, more focused on protecting me. It reminds me of our journey to the Great Green Sea and how Petros the Wise and Serena defended all who were under their protection.

"No bones were broken. The wounds will heal, but he needs rest," the healer says.

Bakiri and our host exchange looks. "We will talk more later. Rest and recover yourself."

In the way of men they go to where the war mares rest and talk quietly to each other. All others stay back and let their elders consult.

The Golden One is helped to a room where he will be protected and quiet. His eyes meet mine. I go with them, and stay while he sinks into a healing sleep. When he moves in his sleep, he groans. I put my fingers on his lips. "Hush," I say. "You are safe. Sleep deeply and recover."

He seems to hear for he quieted. His lips soften under my fingers; it seems that his whole being softens. I do not want to take my fingers away, but want only to keep them there.

Chapter Fifteen

War with the Unknown

Uneasy, I cannot resume my slumbers. Another comes to guard The Golden One. I lie awake—tense, starting at each small noise, wondering which small rustling means danger. My host moves me from the solitary room I have occupied onto the roof where it is cooler. I am surrounded by the women of the household. Like Bakiri, he prefers to concentrate on the war mares that he breeds and trains, but when troubles come to him, as they now do, he has to put aside what really interests him to tend to the protection of his household.

At last the night lifts with the coming of the reborn sun, or so the people of the Land of the One River believe. The noises of the awakening household follow the quiet of the night. The young men who have been guarding us during the long night come one by one to the household to eat lightly, exchange quiet talk and then resume their patrols.

I descend from the roof to see what this day will bring and to hear what the night has brought to my new friends.

"You will not return to the school. It is too dangerous," Bakiri says to me, which is no surprise.

I reply, "I thought as much. I learned all I could there. I wasted no time."

The Golden One joins us and hears my response to Bakiri. He looks at me. I look at him. He moves with some stiffness. Bruises make purple splotches against his fair skin. His wounds are healing well, with no signs of red or swelling.

Speaking to Bakiri he says, "I thank you for the care you gave me last night. I think it is time that I returned to he who brought me to this land. He resides with friends near the shop of the worker of gold. I, too, have learned what I was sent to learn, and perhaps will be permitted to start my journey back to the land of my people."

"Why were you sent to the school?" our host asks him. In other times it might be discourteous to ask such a question of a guest, but given that he was attacked and then came here to warn us, the usual courtesies can be ignored.

"It was thought I should become familiar with the dance and the music taught at the school. It was also thought that I would be safer tucked away far from the city. It was not so," the Golden One replies.

"Do you know why you were attacked?" Bakiri questions him.

"No one would talk to me before Alimah joined the classes. But I did not sense danger, just distrust from my looking so different from the others. They suspected I was one of the sea peoples, which I am not, and disliked me because of that. But when Alimah joined us, there was a change from distrust to outright hostility. I don't know why, for they never said. Or they said in such rapid words that

64

I could not follow, which they well knew. So I don't know why." The Golden One ceases talking.

My guardians join in. Fahim says, "I knew some of the students' older brothers and sisters. When I talked to them they were wary of Alimah and The Golden One and could not say why, or from whom the talk came from. They are young and noticed not, just accepted. They recognized the great gifts of Alimah and, in the way of the young and not very gifted, disliked her. They also disliked her because she worked so hard and learned so much, so swiftly."

He pauses and then continues, "The Golden One fascinated them, but again they didn't know from whom the hostility towards him came from. They shrugged their shoulders and professed ignorance. Again, they are young, and not acquainted with the ways of their elders. Not interested either." The last is uttered with contempt because he thinks that not only are they young but they are far too silly for their ages.

Bakiri and our host look at each other. "Well," Bakiri says, "as my other self, Petros the Wise, would do, we shall take these two who seem to be targets for someone away from here and try to get both to a place of safety."

He turns to The Golden One. "We would escort you to your people. Does that meet with your approval?"

"Yes," he replies. "I thank you for your courtesy and for your protection. I no longer have need to remain here, and now every reason to leave."

Chapter Sixteen

We Journey Again

We wait for The Golden One to heal before we leave on our next journey. Bakiri learns what he can from him, trying to do so in a manner that will not alarm him.

"We will be riding when we leave here. We need to pick a war mare for you," Bakiri says.

The Golden One caresses the nose of the light grey war mare picked for him. They eye each other. He slides onto her back, and they meld into one as she carries him swiftly around the pasture. Her silver tail arches and flows behind her and his golden hair flows and shines, mingling with her mane as he bends over her arched neck in the bright sun. They shine, giving off sparks of gold and silver, his long golden legs encircling her round body. She, the war mare, exalts in being let loose to run freely with her golden rider, as joyous as she. Suddenly we see that he is upright, his feet on her moving back, his body proudly swaying in rhythm with hers. *His display is for me,* I think. Just as a bird will display bright feathers for she whom he wishes as a mate, this display is for me. I thrill at it. It is a sight that will stay with me forever.

The display also scares me. The Golden One is claiming me, by claiming my eyes on him.

Bakiri and our host are astonished at the Golden One's knowledge of the war mares. The Golden One has passed one test. He appears to know it, for his blue eyes gleam as he sees the look on Bakiri's face. Then his face shuts down as if he has let some knowledge slip that is dangerous.

The young men test him in the use of daggers and other arms. He passes their tests, also. They acknowledge him as one who has led warriors. He picks the best daggers to conceal about his person. To me he has always seemed a warrior who looks out of place in a school devoted to the arts of song and dance. It is as if he had discarded garments that suited him not and now shows himself as the young leader he is meant to be.

Bakiri speaks to me. "I wonder why his people hid him in the school for the arts, for he is destined to lead his people. I see no reason for him to be there. Is he gifted in song and dance, Alimah?"

"Yes and no, Bakiri," I reply, uneasy.

Bakiri's dark eyes almost snap at me. "Yes and no! What does that mean, Alimah?" The edge in his voice is quite clear to me.

"Yes, in that he approached the dance and the songs and the instruments to learn them, and learn them he did, and very well, too. No, in that the desire to learn them does not burn in him, drive him to learn more and more and better and better. It is as if he is learning how to use a tool, like a dagger, or riding one of the war mares."

Bakiri's voice loses its snap. "Ah, I see what you mean. He is not a gifted one as you know the gifted ones to be. And as I am learning about. I did not understand the gifted ones which is why Salama had to leave here and follow Petros the

Younger into the far lands. My heart grows heavy knowing that I failed her. I will not let that happen again."

"Yes, Bakiri. I see that you understand." My heart full, I smile at him.

"I am learning much from you Alimah," he admits. Very few men can admit that they learn from females or the young.

I bow my head and reply, "And I from you, Bakiri."

"Does the Golden One tell you of his people? I do not ask in idle curiosity but because I sense danger and mysteries." He pauses and continues, almost talking to himself, "I wish Petros the Wise were here. But he is not and I will have to do the best I can."

"No, he says very little. He is careful and hides much about his people and about himself." As if I were betraying my new friend, the Golden One, I say, "He recognized the beads that I wear that came from the Land of the Two Rivers."

"Did he say anything?"

"No, but I could tell by his flash of surprise when he noticed them. He wanted to lean closer and study them, but did not. I know not why. It could have been manners, it could have been that he did not want to betray knowledge of where the beads came from. Serena taught me a lot about reading what those around me are thinking or feeling."

"You seem to think the beads are important." Bakiri studies my calm face.

"Yes, I think so, but I know not why. It puzzles me."

Bakiri again studies me. "It will come to you, Alimah. I have learned that much about the gifted ones. To wait and listen carefully." His face saddens. "If I had listened to Salama she might not have made her perilous journey alone."

Then his face lights up. "If she had not, I might never have known Petros the Wise and his sister Serena. My life would not have been as rich if that had been so. So I have learned to not lament what cannot be changed."

Chapter Seventeen

Journey to the Street of Artisans

The next morning, Bakiri, the Golden One and I with our band of protectors travel down the dusty road to find the Golden One's family and perhaps safety. Our host sends many of his young warriors with us. Every day brings more danger and every day our band of protectors grows larger. All are quiet and vigilant, looking about us, noticing the quiet of the countryside and that the birds are not singing. We are all aware that danger surrounds us and can come upon us at any moment. We need to be alert at all times. We have many long days before we will reach our destination.

Bakiri tells me that the dusty trails used to be much safer. There are now spots that are very unsafe. Our host's neighbors have suffered greatly from raids by those who thrive on chaos. Even though the full force of the Great Destruction has not quite reached the Land of the One River, it has unsettled enough peoples and ways of life that the safety formerly taken for granted is no longer. Like ripples from a stone tossed into a quiet pond, the Great Destruction has disturbed the quiet of the Pharaoh's land.

Desperate hungry peoples have drifted in, attracted by the safety and the reliable crops. As is the way, these new peoples disturb the very safety they are eager for. Food that has been sufficient for life grows scarce, which disturbs the safety even more.

Bakiri's grim face as he recounts these changes in his land saddens me. Everywhere we have been the changes that the Great Destruction has wrought are seen: beauty destroyed, crops destroyed, and people destroyed.

"The old ways are passing and it is unclear what the new ways will bring," he says sadly. "It is hard to know what to do other than bring up our young ones to be strong and to defend our families and our ways of life until we can do no more. I worry, Alimah. I worry. So much will vanish, to be replaced by what?"

"Uncle, has it ever been different? I heard about Thutmose and Hasna who also faced hard times, and danger."

"Alimah, when I see you and those like you, I do not worry so much." He smiles down at me. I think how fond I have become of him.

The Golden One and I ride side by side. I keep an eye on him to be sure that he is not still too stiff to ride for a long distance. He has healed quickly, the purple splotches have faded already. But still, I feel compelled to keep an eye on him. I have noticed, in my own journeys, that no one—men or women—will give in to sickness or fatigue: that no one will admit when they are unable to keep up. From observing the herds of goats and sheep I know it is the same. The weak, who are the easy prey of predators, try to keep up with the herd where safety lies. It seems to be the same with our kind.

71

"Bakiri and his host are curious about you and where you come from, whose people you come from," I say to him.

"I know," he replies. "I can tell you much, but not everything. I cannot put my people in danger."

"You come from far away?" I ask. "I, also, come from far away, but perhaps not as far as you."

"I come from a far away land where my looks are not strange." He pauses and then, singing softly so none could hear but me, resumes.

"Where the days and nights become so cold that the water turns solid and can be walked upon

Where we wear the skins of animals to keep our bodies warm.

When the cold comes, the sun vanishes except for its glow over the horizon.

Where when the weather turns warm the sun never leaves the sky and there is no night."

"We live near a great sea that is like the Great Green Sea. We venture out on it with great joy. Great danger bestows great joy on our kind. We sing of our honorable deeds." His eyes, those eyes that are so strange to me, look out over the fields baking under the hot sun, yet seem to see them not.

I wonder if he has just given me part of a great song cycle.

I say quietly, "I know of the Great Green Sea and traveled along it to reach our destination, although I have never been on it, just near it. We traveled many moons to reach it from where my people live. I have heard from visitors many wondrous tales of the cold that never stops."

He looks down at me. "Do your people live along a trade route?"

I reply, "Once we lived in Ugarit, that is no more. Once we lived closer to The Land of the One River. Our revered ancestor, Thutmose, was Master of Works for the heretic Pharaoh, so we came from the Land of the One River, but have not lived here for many generations. None of my kin now living remember living in the Land of the One River. Bakiri, who is of our blood, was of the ones who stayed here. It is a long story how we came to be in the Land of the One River again, and has to do with a blood feud and the war mares."

He looks interested. "Can you tell it to me? Are you allowed?"

A spurt of anger comes over me as I answer him. "You think I might not be allowed because I am female? Or because I am young? Or because I am one of the gifted ones?"

He looks startled at my anger and replies, "No, none of those. My people here tell nothing of themselves and their stories because of the danger that is all around us. We keep ourselves mysterious, giving nothing away to those who might be our enemies and use the knowledge to harm us."

My anger vanishes as quickly as the storms that come from the Great Green Sea. "So you felt the danger in the school that teaches the arts of song and dance before I came?"

His face shuts down. "Yes," he says softly.

I continue, determined to learn from him, determined to protect myself and all of us with knowledge. If we cannot learn more, how can we protect ourselves and him?

"Bakiri and I both sensed something dangerous the first day when we looked at the classes and the pupils. It disturbed us both. That is why I was brought each day with protectors and returned, escorted by guards, to our hosts every night. We thought the danger was aimed at me." I pause. "Neither of us knew why."

"It was aimed at you, Alimah, but it was there before you came. I know not why or from whom." He studies the fields around us, always alert, although seemingly relaxed.

"Was it because you came from a far away land and looked different?" I ask.

"You do not look different and you come from a far away land," he says with a glint in his eye.

I think it over. He is right. "We don't know enough, do we? Bakiri and I were aware of something dangerous in the school but we knew no more. Our host, when we told him, believed us but did not know why. Your coming to us beaten and injured swept away any doubts that danger resided there, even if the cause was still obscure."

"We, you and I, may have stumbled into something that is very dangerous and has very little to do with us. Some person may seek to use us to gain power or favor, or something." His face tightened. "I do not like being used."

"Neither do I." Angry again, I say, "I remained here to learn the arts of song and dance so that I could return to my people with them as a gift. That is all. That is enough."

His mouth relaxes—the first real sign of softening I have seen in him. "Yes, I see that. You were not sent to befriend me, then."

"Do you mean right now when we are riding together, or do you mean at the school?" I ask, confused and ready to be angry.

"Both or either. I have to be very careful and wary of all who talk to me," he says with no more emotion than if talking about nothing important.

Taking a deep breathe I reply, "I had never heard of you and I was sent only to learn the arts that I needed to learn."

I think to myself, *I do not have to be wary of Bakiri and his family. For they are family. It must be a hard loneliness to be where one can rely on no one. Serena's stories of her times across The Great Green Sea remind me that she was alone for long periods of time and had to protect her children from enemies. It marked her. Even now it marks her.*

"I think that you speak the truth, as you know it. But there could always be someone who uses you." He looks grim.

"Yes," I reply. "I have heard of such. But Bakiri is not such a person. I have not known him long, but I have known him during dangerous events and have seen how he acts. Our host I do not know. But Bakiri has known him." My voice falters, for I am no longer as sure as I am when anger surges in me. There is so much I do not know. I must talk to Bakiri. I have never before had so much to keep secret from so many people. Always before I was protected as a child, as a gifted one, as a female. That protection is being peeled off, layer by layer. I can no longer unthinkingly rely on it. The less I know the more I am in danger.

Chapter Eighteen

Bakiri and Alimah talk

"The Golden One and I have talked, Bakiri. He is wary that I am being used to get either information or something from him. He says that he sensed the danger before I arrived at the school but that it was aimed at him. After I arrived it was aimed at both of us. I do not understand."

Bakiri looks down at me. "Power."

I look my surprise. "Power?" I wonder what power I could possibly have. "I have no power."

"You are graceful in men's eyes. That gives you power. Some try to control anything that will lead them to have more power. Sometimes it is the ear of those who rule. Sometimes it is other forms of power. Anyone who controls the trade routes, or the war mares, or the bright stones that make men and women greedy, has power and wants to use it for their own purposes." Bakiri gives me a sad smile. "Those, like myself, who only want to be let alone to breed and train war mares, are forced to think about those who desire power. We have to protect ourselves so we do not become used by clever men."

Perhaps Petros the Wise knows Bakiri's views but this is the first I have heard of them. Perhaps that is why those two, who are alike enough to be brothers, exchange their views of power. Bakiri almost lost his cherished war mares to evil and an old family feud, and has to think these thoughts so that he and his are never in that jeopardy again.

I stay in this land only to learn the arts of song and dance and of the stringed instruments. Sardow, the gifted one before my time, said that she had to be out on the dangerous streets of Ugarit to collect images. Hoval had to hold the gems in his hands before he could bring out all their beauty. I wonder if Petros the Wise foresaw that I would learn of the ways of men and power if I stayed here without Serena or Kaliq to protect me. I had thought to be like the birds in the trees singing with no other thoughts, but I had not considered that the birds have to protect their young and themselves from danger and predators. I am learning that I have to protect myself and my gifts.

"I will not willingly be some other's tool," I proclaim through gritted teeth.

"I know, Alimah, but sometimes we can not control everything. Sometimes without knowing it we are others' tools. All we can do is be alert and true to ourselves."

"Bakiri, do you have any idea who or what is stirring and making our lives dangerous?"

"No. I would guess and say it has to do with trade and the trade routes. Especially since the Golden One is also aware of danger. Unlike the war mares, the stones that glitter and can be shaped are small and easily transported in secret. I noticed that the Golden One has stones on him that were shaped in the Land of the Two Rivers. Some golden stones from far away have been used in the heretic Pharaoh's ornaments. They are called the Gold of the North."

"Should we both inquire of The Golden One?" I ask him, afraid that the answer will be yes. Something in me does not want to disturb the growing understanding between The Golden One and me.

"I think not. He does not have enough reasons to trust us. We will wait until we can restore him to his people."

Relieved. For the first time in many days I wish to let out a song into the warm air, to let it loose among the growing plants, to let it loose into the fragrance that is this strange land. Aware that danger surrounds us, however, I keep my mouth closed just like the birds do when they sense danger is near.

Days pass as we continue on our journey. The Golden One by now is completely healed. Sometimes he rides at my side, sometimes amongst the protectors, absorbing all that they know as they absorb what he knows of war and danger. At night we stay in compounds of another of the People of the Horse. We can let down our guard, for all of the compounds are defended well by grim young men. The Great Destruction and the chaos that comes in its wake has reached further into the Land of the One River than we had known.

Our hosts are most concerned about their source of fresh war mares rather than the trade routes that move fine jewelry, perfumes and other easily transported goods. But they are coming to see that they, too, have to be concerned about the trade routes, for the same trade routes are used to refresh the stock of war mares and perhaps, bring a superior stallion, to the Land of the One River. It is clear that the disruption of the trade routes affects everyone.

On we ride in the hot sun. Bakiri and the others know where we are going. So do the protectors, for if something happens to our leaders, the protectors will have to take charge.

Chapter Nineteen

We Reach Our Destination

We ride into the narrow streets that I have heard about from my kin. They had seemed myth, but now they are not. The rough cobblestones, the fetid alleys, the many boats that line the great river, all these I have heard of. The dangers that lurk in these narrow streets lined with the shops of those who make fine goods have been part of my kin's stories.

"You know of the old gold worker?" That The Golden One recognizes our destination is a surprise. Startled, I remember the stories I have heard. First, about our ancestor Hoval and then about the three brothers whom I know: Petros the Younger, Diripi and Arudara, who came here not so long ago. Because it was becoming too dangerous for them to remain here in the Land of the One River, the old gold maker sent some of his youngsters back with the three brothers of the kin. They told us stories of their old home.

The Golden One whispers urgently to me, "You have heard of him?"

"Yes, he is well known in my kin. Some of the gifted ones have been gifted in the making of jewelry that pleases those in power. How do you know of him?"

His face closes again. I will not get an answer. Bakiri must have been right about the trade routes and the gems.

Quickly I put together seemingly odd facts. When first I appeared at the school I wore around my neck the beads that are from my kin. The beads have the northern gold, as well as the bright blue lapis that comes from the far ends of the trade route we live along. Arudara, gifted in gems, had put them together for me and bestowed it upon me at our leaving. I had thought little of it for I am used to always wearing it.

I remember The Golden One also wore jewelry that came not only from the Land of the One River. The beads he wore came also from the Land of the Two Rivers and I noticed some of the gold of the north.

Before I can stop myself I say to him, "We both wear jewelry that does not come from this land. It marks us. Maybe that is the source of the danger." I wish immediately that I had not said that.

His features become even more immobile as he frowns at me. "Shush, Alimah! It is not always safe to say out loud whatever you are thinking."

I feel like shouting at him, but do not. It comes to me then that being the mate of a powerful man will mean that I will have to watch my every word, be very careful with everyone. Eyes will be watching, ears will catch every utterance and, as jewelers keep every bit of gold because it is valuable, onlookers will store up each scrap of information. I sigh. So much to learn before I can be a worthy mate to

Kaliq, my intended one. I wish for Serena—she would know the answers. But, as she said to me, if I learned it myself it would be in me and never be lost or forgotten.

At the sight of our group the street empties. The night blinds over the store fronts are lowered. All is quiet, for our well-armed troop means danger to those on the street. Still, I am aware of eyes upon us, measuring us, perhaps weighing how much could be gained by selling such knowledge to those who are our enemies.

A quiet conversation between Bakiri and the man at the door of the shop and then Bakiri vanishes inside. He comes out and motions us to follow him. He murmurs the directions he has been given to one of the young warriors with us, who has a flash of surprise on his face. Off we ride again. Quickly. It will bring danger to this street if our large group of well-armed men dallies here. No one talks. I say no more. The Golden One says no more.

Chapter Twenty

More Mysteries

We ride into the courtyard of yet another walled country house. The sun is still arcing in the high, pristine sky, the animals and people somnolent under the harsh light. Even the donkeys stand drooping in the heat. Our war mares are not subdued but prance along on dainty hooves, their tails arched in the way of their kind.

We are greeted by many men garbed in desert coverings; their beards and flowing coverings set them apart from the men of the Land of the One River. I am by now used to seeing men who never wear beards and rarely have hair on their heads. Wigs are commonly used when coverings of the head are necessary. The scanty clothes commonly worn in the heat of the Land of the One River no longer startle me into wondering where my eyes should rest. So much brown skin showing no longer makes me uneasy. That was another way the Golden One and I were set apart at the school. We both kept the hair on our heads. We learned, however, to bathe frequently as those who came from the Land of the One River did. The heat and the insects made that a pleasure.

I stare at two of the bearded men. Surely I do not recognize them, for they do not look as they did when last I saw them.

"Arudara?" I stammer, unsure. "Diripi?"

"We have been expecting you, Alimah." Arudara spoke first, then Diripi spoke. "Greetings from your kin, Alimah. We have heard of your troubles."

The Golden One is enveloped in the desert robes of another bearded one. He is tall like the Golden One, has a red beard and those same strange blue eyes.

He says to the Golden One and to the rest of us, "We have been waiting for Havardr and all the rest of you. Welcome."

I can feel the ways of childhood leaving me with such swiftness that I am giddy. From being one who has been protected at all times, expected to do nothing but learn and perform, now I will learn to act—and my acts will affect others. No longer can I only think of learning new songs, new dances, new ways of performing. I stand straighter and observe all about me. Serena is not there to tell me what is going on, so I have to figure it out for myself. She has taught me well. I draw myself up proudly and gaze about me. Somehow I know that danger is all around us. Danger I am not used to, can barely discern, and understand poorly.

Arudara is gifted with gems, like so many in our kin. Diripi, like his father Lukenow, is a man of the sea and cannot be content when he is far from it. The danger that Havardr—The Golden One—and I both found in the school has its roots in gems, always a dangerous trade—now more dangerous than ever because of the disruptions of the trade routes that come with the Great Destruction.

Bakiri has never met these brothers. When he realizes who these men are, he also realizes that the dangers that menace Havardr and me come from the trading of gems. I can see the understanding wash over his face; his eyes dart at me and I nod to him in agreement.

"I think they, whoever they were, wanted to capture me and force me to tell of the secrets of the trade routes, or maybe they wanted to pretend to exchange me for the valuable gems. I doubt I would have been permitted to live," says Havadr.

"How did they know of the gems and the gold of the north? We thought we had hidden you wisely," inquires the red-bearded one.

Havardr, with color high on his face replies, "Alimah put it together. She noticed that we both had fine jewelry, both from the Land of the Two Rivers and the Land of the One River, on our persons. We also had the northern gold mixed in. Both of us had jewelry ordinarily worn by kings and their consorts. The jewels marked us, marked us as valuable to be captured and traded. Traded as the jewels were, as the war mares have been."

"My necklace was made by Arudara. Those who know gems would recognize it as from a master craftsman," I add quietly. "Those who saw mine and Havardr's would know that it came from far along the ancient trade routes. It made others covet what to us was a memento from where we both came, a reminder of home." I pause, then ask, "I thought that it was too dangerous for Arudara and Diripi to return to the Land of the One River?"

Arudara replies, "I needed gemstones and gold and the Gold of the North."

85

Diripi quietly adds, "I came to keep Arudara company." I know however, that Arudara, as one of the gifted ones, needs protection and that is why Diripi has come with him.

I shudder for I have heard how dangerous it can be if Arudara or Diripi are recognized. I think again to myself, *I stayed here to learn the arts. I did not stay here for adventures. I did not seek adventures. I don't want adventures.*

The red-bearded man says, "Let me show you what I have with me of the Gold of the North. This we can do in a quiet place without drawing dangerous attention. Arudara, come with me and I will show you. We must be swift for all around us is danger—the Gold of the North which I bring makes men mad to possess it."

Arudara and the red-bearded man go to another room. I have heard that Arudara in his mind goes to a far place when looking at uncut gems, some far place where he can see how to bring out the beauty in them. He will be safe with the red-bearded man. Usually Diripi or even Lukenow stands right by him, armed and alert to danger and ready to protect him.

Havardr looks at me. I look at him. The time has come for openness.

"The red-bearded one is your father?" I ask.

"He is my mother's brother," he replies.

"He trades in gems?"

"The Gold of the North is very valuable. As are other small items that are easily transported," he replies, finally meeting my eyes.

"You will lead your people when you return?" I asked again, not willing to let this part remain mysterious.

"Yes, it is the way of my people. It is also the way of my people that I should travel along the trade routes and know danger," he adds, almost unwillingly.

"You have to be tested before you can lead your people." I did not ask the question. I assumed it. It is the way of many peoples—not my kin, who are tested in other ways, but many other peoples.

"Yes," he replies. Then, as if the words come out unwillingly, "My mate comes from a warrior family of much renown. We need to have strong sons to follow me."

I say carefully, "My kin is different from yours. We have the traders and the warriors as your people do. We also have the gifted ones who are protected and cherished, men and women both. Our mating is different, too."

He stares at me. "I cannot go where my hearts desire takes me. I have duties to my people."

I stare back. "I know. I see. I, also, have duties to my kin. Not the same as yours, but duties."

I want a golden-haired child to take back to my kin. What hard choice will this desire lead me to? What sorrows will come from this desire? My gifts, what will happen to my gifts? All is in turmoil. Where my path has been clear, now it is not.

Chapter Twenty-One

More Dangers

"Diripi," I ask, "how did you hear of our adventures?"

"Lukenow sent a messenger to tell all of us. The messenger reached us before Petros the Wise and all under his protection reached us. We went to the Bedouins and they mounted us on valiant steeds to make our journey swifter. Arudara and I set out and grew our disguises as we came, so that by the time we reached the Land of the One River no one could recognize us as the same men who came here not long ago."

"I thought it too dangerous for you and Arudara to return to the Land of the One River?" I say, concerned for their safety.

"We came well disguised and since we had been here before we were familiar with the streets where we had escaped those who hunted us. More experienced, this time we could evade the dangers that surrounded us. The old gold worker and his sons know we are allies and can help us. So we came here knowing who we could rely upon."

Diripi is keeping something from me. Something he thinks is important. I could stomp my foot in exasperation but, newly emerged from my childish ways, I realize that

I cannot. To be listened to I have to prove that I am fully grown and can be trusted.

"Diripi, what of those who returned with Petros the Wise? Are they all in good health—Serena, Lukenow, The Bedouin, Dalil, Kaliq?" I will have to be persistent to get the news I need.

Diripi, so good at keeping a calm face when on the seas or when guarding Arudara, has trouble meeting my eyes. Is there some bad news he does not want me to know? How ridiculous. He is a protector but he is taking it too far. I am not a fragile being who hears unexpected news and crumbles to the ground. I stare at him with my face implacable and hard.

He squirms and then says, "We heard of their many adventures. They found a sick girl and protected her until she was well. Her name is Leila. Dalil and Leila are well suited and they are now mated. Alimah, it was well known that you and Dalil might have been fated for each other."

I reply, more curtly than I intend, "No, we were not. We could not see into each others hearts and realized it. He is my kin and I am glad that he has found someone. Did Kaliq also find someone on that long journey?"

Diripi replies with his usual kindness, "No, Alimah. He learns the arts of leadership from Petros the Wise. He rides with him, talks with him, and fights with him against those who attack us. He spends all his time learning from him. That is all I heard before Arudara and I left."

I am glad that Kaliq has found no one, for I wish to return to him. Then I remember that I also wish to return with a golden-haired child: a tall, strong, golden- haired child. How can I wish for Kaliq as my mate, as my companion for life, if I also wish for a golden-haired child?

I look at Bakiri and realize that he is listening closely to something I hear not. Perhaps I will never hear for this is not my land. I open my mouth to question, but he silences me with a quick gesture. In an instant I am taken to another room and quickly swathed in desert robes and told to act the part of a young man. Havardr is whisked away to where I know not. I know enough to not protest or try to speak.

Hustled out the back door, my protector is knocked to the ground as a strange set of hands grabs me. I see the scarred face of he who hunted Havardr. I start to yell, but his sweaty, fetid hand clamps over my mouth, stifling my sounds. I have learned much as I studied the dance. I slump against him, a dead weight, and when he tries to scoop me up, I wriggle away, draw my dagger and aim it at the hand that still grasps me.

"Quiet!" the brutal voice growls in my ear. "It will go easier with you if you do not struggle." I do not believe it for I can feel his man's arousal against me. I can smell his excitement and his rage. Although terrified, I know I have to be like Kaliq and keep my wits about me, to let my other protectors know where I am and that I am in danger.

As I plunge my dagger into his grimy hand, I make the sounds that the desert hunting birds make when signaling danger. My captor swears, but his hand lets go of me as blood gushes from the wound. He turns, bares his teeth, and draws his dagger to avenge my insult to him. I struggle and use my dancer's body to slither away from him, to evade him and his terrible lust. I hear myself gasping for breath, for my strength is no match to his. I feel myself weakening but keep on resisting until I can be rescued.

My Bedouin protectors come with the stealth of the desert birds who pounce on their prey and tear it apart with lethal talons. He is overwhelmed as I am seized by one of our desert friends. I see not what becomes of him. I hope my friends send him to his ancestors.

Thrown onto the back of a war mare, I am led swiftly away. Where all has been terror and confusion, now all is purposeful and quiet as we ride away from the grim scene. The winds keep us cool until the moon lights our way. We are all silent. I am safe with the men of the Great Desert, kin of The Bedouin. I see their faces and recognize some of them. They move silently, more silently than any of the Land of the One River or even the Land of the Two Rivers. The war mares also are silent, as they are trained to be.

I hear disturbing sounds from behind us: sounds of horses that are not war mares, who are quiet, always. Perhaps the scarred one is one of many and they are pursuing us. I will have bruises from the rough handling. But, I think with satisfaction, *the scarred one will have more than bruises.* I swallow my tears—now is not the time for them. Maybe later I can let them fall.

On we ride. I worry about Arudara and Diripi for I do not see them in our company. I worry about Bakiri who has become as another father to me, and is also not with us. I worry about Havardr and his red-bearded uncle who are not with us. I imagine them hurt or gone to be with their ancestors and grieve that I could not even say my farewells to them.

We ride until the golden orb sinks low in the sky to its daily death. On we ride in the moonlight—we never stop, never eat, moving as the men of the desert move, needing neither food nor water nor rest. Silent we ride, silent we remain.

We reach another great house with a courtyard and stables. Silent, we enter through the gate at the front, and ride to the stables. One of the men of the desert tucks me under his arm and hustles me through a window into a small room. He puts his fingers to his lips when I open my mouth to question. He whispers in my ear, "Stay quiet! We have to make sure of your safety. Stay here."

Another comes silently through the window. I catch a glimpse. It is Havardr. He, too, is left with the same instructions.

Speechless, still, we look at each other. His eyebrows are raised. Seeing the look on my face, he folds me into his arms. I can feel his warmth through the desert robes, can feel his young, hard muscles. His hand soothes me, travels down my back. I do not realize it but I am trembling, shaking.

I now have time to clean my dagger. He looks on as I do so, his face showing nothing, but his eyes widen. With a few quick motions, I wipe away the blood that defaces it.

A man garbed in the robes of the desert comes silently in, draws Havardr aside and murmurs to him in a tongue I know not. It is not the speech of the Bedouin with which I am familiar, but another speech. I wonder if it comes from that far away place that Havardr comes from. He, the man, gives me a look and then departs.

Havardr draws me back into his arms and whispers into my ear, in such a low voice that none but I can hear. "We will stay in this room until it is clear that the danger is over. Things are confused; it is hard to know who, among those of this land, is our enemy and who is not. We will stay hidden until events clarify themselves."

I whisper back, "I am worried about my kin."

"I am worried about mine. There is no news."

"This is all about the gems, is it not?"

He softly replies, "I think so, but am not sure."

Backs to the wall, we sit together on the floor. I wonder how Serena stood it when she and The Bedouin were prisoners in a small room. They knew they were in terrible danger as prisoners of the Evil One. We are not prisoners but are shielded from danger. Havardr is not alarmed so I will not be alarmed. We are both worried about those dear to us, but our task is to wait.

When I awaken, the moon light makes stripes on the floor and the walls as sweet night smells waft through the window. Havardr's arm is around me, holding me close to him. His firm mouth is in a grim line, his daggers close at hand. A shadowy form comes in the window. Quietly we both rise. In the next instant I am trapped behind Havadr, as he wields a dagger in each hand, ready to defend us.

"Ppstt," the form says in the northern tongue. They both bundle me out the window as we make our silent way to where the war mares stand ready. Once again, I am flung onto the back of my war mare and off we ride out the back of the stables, down a narrow dusty trail, the moon shining down on us. Havardr rides behind me as I follow him who has summoned us out the window. On we ride, quiet as thieves, quiet as the predator hawks, quiet as the big cats who hunt their prey, on and on in the silvery moonlight.

It seems a dream, but the quiet dainty footsteps of the war mares tell me it is not a dream—and when I look back and see the shadowed face of Havardr, I know it is not a dream.

At last we pause, turn down a short, hidden lane and arrive at yet another courtyard and stables. Havardr catches me as I slide off of the war mare and holds me close to him. We climb onto the roof above the stables, the moon lighting our way. We hear the rustlings of the war mares below us, inhale the sweet scents of the night. All is calm. He draws me down onto a palette, holds me close and says in the tongue of the Land of the One River, "Sleep. You are safe. Sleep."

I sleep. I might never see my kin again. He is all I know from my old life. I am a child no longer.

Chapter Twenty-Two

Alimah Awakens

I hear the birds, I hear the rustling of the war mares beneath us: morning sounds. The sun has not yet made its appearance, but the dark is yielding to the soft colors that herald the new day.

Opening my eyes, I turn over and look directly into the blue eyes of Havardr. The hairs on his face glow red in the coming light. He reaches out a finger and traces it along my face, down my neck. A light hand caresses my shoulder then makes its way down my body.

"Alimah," his voice rasps. His hands grasp me and hold me tight against his body, his aroused body. "I cannot resist."

His body covers mine. I do not resist, cannot resist any more than he can. I meet him, ready and eager. I have no thought for duties to my kin, for my kin are absent and I know not if or when I will ever rejoin them. He is here, his life-giving force is here. I can no longer turn away from it or him. This is release and life after all the dangers we have been through together.

Perhaps this morning we make the golden-haired child I dream of.

95

Chapter Twenty-Three

Our Dangerous Journey Continues

We both tidy ourselves before one of our desert friends silently appears. In his hands he holds some dates and some bread for sustenance. We hurry for he is clearly impatient. I want to touch Havardr but restrain myself. Our safety might depend upon my not revealing my feelings.

Again, on our war mares we ride and ride and ride. I am not so comfortable as the day before, for that part of myself lets me know that it has never before been used that way. Gradually, fatigue makes me forget the small twinges of muscles. Havardr quickly covers up his look of concern, as I cover up the small discomforts of being on the war mare's back.

We come to yet another walled compound; I have no idea where in the Land of the One River we are. I worry about Bakiri, so dear to me. I worry about my protectors whom I had become used to during the time I spent at the school. I can do nothing about my worries.

This is how Havardr lived at the school, I realize. Alone, perpetually alone and having to be alert to every nuance in a language that he is not fluent in. He must have, as I had to, learned to read faces and to read what was in the minds of those who surrounded him. I wonder if this is the way I will live always, surrounded by strangers and by dangers I understand not.

We leave our war mares at the stables and make our weary way to the door that stands open to us. We are greeted by Bakiri and the red-bearded man. I fall into Bakiri's firm clasp and hold tight, trying not to shake. He gently pushes me away from him, hands on my shoulders, concern in his face.

"Alimah, are you all right? The days have been long since last I saw you."

"Uncle, I am all right. I was worried about you." I force a smile for him.

His keen eyes look at me and spare a glance for Havardr. "No one has used you roughly?"

"No, Bakiri, no one has used me roughly," I reply. "Where are we, what is going on? Who has been taking us from place to place?" Questions tumble out of me.

He replies, "We who breed and take care of the war mares form a tight friendship. We are as brothers and defend not only the war mares but our families from those who mean us harm. We keep the best war mares from Pharaoh's army. We trade the best stallions among us so as to improve the next generation of war mares. No one who is not of us is admitted into our confidences." He pauses, then continues, "The Bedouin, the people of the desert, are our friends if we treat the war mares well. Those who do not, become their

97

enemies. They care not about the gems that adorn both men and women, for their life in the desert is simple and austere. Life under the stars and fighting is what they enjoy. Not for them the arts that you came to learn. But they are our friends and we can rely upon them."

"What has caused all the troubles? The war mares?"

"No, it is the gems and the trade routes. Gems that can be hidden and carried from place to place. Arudara and Diripi came here to acquire gems for Arudara to work with. The Gold of the North is as valuable as the gold that comes from the Land of the One River, which they also seek. Arudara needs all of the gems and gold for his work. It is very hard to leave this land with valuables and Pharaoh keeps very careful track of the gold that men covet. But," Bakiri smiles, "there are ways. Just as there are ways to conceal the best war mares. It is dangerous and tricky."

"Diripi and Arudara?" I question him. Surely if they have been injured or captured Bakiri will tell me.

"They have completed what they came here to do. They will leave soon. I am thinking that we might want to send you back with them. What think you? Have you learned what you set out to?"

I am honored that Bakiri asks my opinion. No longer a child, I have changed in his eyes, too.

Bakiri continues, his face troubled. "It will take some time to take you and Havardr to the Great Green Sea where you can depart unnoticed. Diripi and Arudara will come back in several moons to pick you up. There will be less danger if you leave gradually and not from the Great River where so many eyes can see you. You and Havardr are being hunted by many, for the Gold of the North is very valuable.

A price has been put on your heads. There is much talk of the two of you."

I consider for a moment then say, "I think it would be best to leave for I cannot learn the new ways of song and dance when I am being hunted and in danger. I have learned much in my time here, perhaps there is no more to learn."

There are the arts of the Land of the Two Rivers and even farther along the trade routes, lands that seem incredible to think about that I might learn from. Havardr and I inhabited a dream on top of those stables, but it was a dream. What of my wish for a golden-haired child? My mind shies away from that. I cannot think of that now. Not yet.

Chapter Twenty-Four

We Journey With the Men of the Great Desert

Serena has taught me much about the men who live in the Great Desert with their camels and their war mares. The war mares live in the tents with the women and children, so they are not easily stolen. The war mares are bred to be docile and sweet tempered, as well as to be valiant in the raids that their masters so enjoy. The Bedouin women are not treated as the women of the kin are treated, but that is not unusual, for our kin's ways with women and children and the gifted ones are different than any whom we have knowledge of.

Serena spoke of how hard it would be for one of our kin to live among them and be one with them. She told me how Petros the Younger had been frustrated in his desire to help the women bring children into being, for he knew he could help and was not allowed to. Serena had a far away look on her as she told me the tales. I could not help but notice, without noticing, how the eyes of The Bedouin were drawn again and again and again to Serena. I wonder if she turned to him when they were captured and threatened. She greeted Lukenow's return with joy and maybe relief? I wonder anew, as I remember the events of that time.

Would I ever have lain with Havardr if we had not been in the midst of dangers? We had looked into each others minds and hearts when we were both students of the dance and singing and of the instruments that make glorious sounds. He taught me the arts of the Bull Dancers and we practiced them together. He is not a gifted one as my kin knows them. He is something different: a warrior.

It is the jewels that encircle both of our necks that draws others' ill attentions. We wear our jewels as a reminder of those whom we have left far away. Some, amongst all the people I have heard of, wear the bright stones to impress others with their power. Some wear bright stones because of their beauty. Many, who have not the wealth for the finest of stones and the finest settings, wear simple ornaments to remind them of a father, a mother, a loved one. Thus it is that I wear the necklace that Arudara has made for me. I think it the same for Havardr.

If ever I go on another journey to a strange place, I will be more careful of what I display, what jewels I wear, what clothes I wear, what words I utter, what songs I sing. Something in me rebels at the disguises I may be forced to don. How can I perfect my arts if I have to disguise what I am, constantly?

Then, I remember the stories of Sardow, who went into the dangerous streets of Ugarit, which is no more, disguised as a boy, or disguised as someone she was not. But when she returned to her studio she could drop the disguise and be her own self as she made beauty. The stories say she needed to go out into the streets to harvest images. She could not live isolated and use her gifts well.

Perhaps I can use this pattern. Perhaps the songs I make will stir more hearts because of what I have experienced on this strange trip—what I will experience as this trip continues.

Every day we ride in the midst of the men of the desert and make our way to another walled house. We are roused as the sun comes up and ride until the sun meets its daily demise in the western sky. Every night we are in a different walled house. Sometimes we are left alone in a room in the night. Sometimes Havardr and I are tucked on a roof, where the cool breezes whisper around us. Under the stars that glow at us, we explore each other. The moon has turned from the full to a sliver four times and still we ride on. I am beginning to understand the speech of those with whom we ride. All the fatigue that beset me when first we started out has ceased. I have become used to this life.

All around us is danger, for the times are even more disturbed than we were aware of. We see crops burned. We see the desperate bandits along the lanes, filthy and starved and the more dangerous for that. They live like the feral dogs that feed on the remains of those who have been sent to be with their ancestors. We see small children who are too thin to cry. The smells that accompany these sights seem to stay in our robes and never leave, reminding us always of the sights we have seen. I begin to understand that the Great Destruction is not mere words but something vicious let out on many lands.

I want to turn my head and not see these sights but that is not possible. I see Havardr looking more grim every day. I wish to be in his arms and shed tears, but that is not possible.

Havardr and I do not touch during the day; we do not speak for we ride quietly with our silent companions through the Land of the One River. Only when we are alone do we speak and touch, holding each other as if another day will never come, touching each other as if we may go to be with our ancestors before another day expires, and trying always to forget the sights that have come to haunt us.

We are always greeted as friends as we stay each night in a different compound with those who are of the brotherhood who protect and cherish the war mares.

Chapter Twenty-Five

We Bid Farewell to the Land of the One River

The men of the desert, who have swiftly taken us from one place to another, lead us across the sands that protect the Land of the One River. It is seemingly barren, but not to those who know how to survive on it. They and the war mares seem more relaxed as we cross the barrier. When last I came this way there was a sandstorm. We had to halt and wait until it ceased. We were pursued by enemies that time, and we are pursued by enemies this time. I begin to know that I, along with everyone else, will always be in danger from those who mean us ill. But I will continue to sing my songs and use my body to make beauty. It is what I am made for and no one will silence me.

As the desert night falls, we sleep with our heads on the war mares. If we reach up it seems we could gather the stars in our grasping hands, hold them as they slip through our fingers. The sliver of the moon hides low in the night sky.

Havardr speaking softly says, "When I am out on the Great Sea that I live near, the night sky seems as it does here. The stars so close as if I had only to reach out and touch them. There, as here, I know where I am by stars in the sky, know how to get to the next place I am traveling towards."

I move closer to him, for it is chilly in the night. The war mare is warm beneath my head, but the rest of me is covered in light robes. He reaches out his hand to me and I place mine in his.

"This has been a strange journey," I murmur. "I stayed here only to study the ways of the singing of songs and the making of dances. I did learn, but I imagined there would be more to it."

His voice smiled, "And what did you learn here?"

"Not what I expected to," I say sadly. "I don't know where this journey will end."

"I do not know for myself, either. Soon, my uncle and I will start our journey back to our people, bringing with us the goods that we were sent to find." The soft voice continues, "Won't you come with me? With us?"

"How can I?" I ask. "You have a mate waiting for you. I have duties to my own people." I say the magic word, "duties," but how can I go to a far place with him when I would be leaving my own people who have known me and mine my whole life. Serena, Petros the Wise, Dalil, who is now mated to another, and most of all, Kaliq. How can I leave Kaliq whom I meant to spend my life with, have children with?

"Those of us who lead often have more than one mate," he says.

I reply, "In my kin, we have only one mate at a time."

"We belong together, you and I. You know that." His voice comes soft as a desert breeze to my ears.

I swallow hard to make my voice say only what I allow, "We belong together on this journey. I cannot go with you to that other life that you lead. I have duties to my people. I have a duty to my gifts that belong to my people."

"Alimah, you must come with me. You know that you are mine. You know what we have shared. You carry my child." His voice is not pleading but sure that what he says is so.

"I cannot come with you. We have what we have, now." I am near tears.

"I could make you come for I am larger and stronger than you," he says. I hear the tension in his voice.

"Yes, you could, but you will not." I know this as I know the sun will make its way over the horizon.

"How can you know?" he asks again.

"If you forced me to come with you, it would ruin what you want me for. I could no longer sing my songs, or move my body in joyous dance. What would be left of me would not be worth having, and I know that you know this."

"How?" he demands.

"I just know." Tears come, and slide down my cheeks; I weep without sound. His finger touches my wet face. His tender lips touch my wet face. I burrow into the curve of his body, wanting to never leave him, but knowing that we have very little time. Soon we must part.

He sighs. "You are right. I will not force you to come with me. But you will be mine until that time of parting. I will protect you until then, and cherish you, my Alimah."

We sleep the sleep of lovers. I think I shall never forget the feel of the desert air on me, the warmth of the war mare's body, the warmth of Havardr's body and the time that we stepped out of our lives and lived only in the day.

Chapter Twenty-Six

The Great Green Sea

We reach the Great Green Sea and stand at its shores, breathing in the salt air, watching the sea creatures as they play. The sea birds wheel and dive. A familiar boat bobs in the waves off shore. A figure stands upon the deck and waves to us.

Diripi brings the boat to shore and greets me and all of our group. Arudara is with him.

Havardr's uncle, who has rejoined us, greets Diripi and Arudara, but mostly Diripi, for he recognizes Diripi as a fellow warrior and as a man who, like himself, is at home on the sea.

The red-bearded one says to Diripi, "We have brought Alimah to you; we have kept her safe."

"Arudara has made many articles of jewelry for you to take with you on your return journey. As well, he has collected many fine gems for you to take back with you," Diripi replies.

Arudara says, "I will make things of great beauty with the Gold of the North, settings that will enhance their glowing beauty. I have made one necklace especially for The Golden One." He presents to Havardr the necklace that is made of blue lapis beads from beyond the Land of the Two Rivers, the Gold of the North separates the beads, and scattered among them are gold beads from the Land of the One River. It glows in the sunlight, glows against Havardr's golden neck.

Havardr bows his thanks to Arudara.

"Are you ready Alimah?" Diripi asks me.

I take a deep breath, hardly able to speak. "Yes, I am. I will say my fare wells." This is worse than when Petros the Wise left with our people. I say my farewells to the Bedouins who have guarded me so well. I stroke the soft nose of the war mare who has carried me over so many miles. I say goodbye to the red-bearded uncle of Havardr and at last I come to him, my Golden One. I stand speechless, the words stuck in my throat.

"This is not 'goodbye,' Alimah," he says, "it is 'until we meet again'." The sun shines on his golden hair, on his tall, golden body and lights up his eyes that are the color of the sky. He puts out his hand, places it softly on my shoulder and stoops to murmur goodbye to me.

Tears hidden deep inside, I go with Arudara and Diripi and as we sail away, I look back to catch the last sight of Havardr as he stands watching us depart. He becomes smaller and smaller as we sail away. Finally, he is hidden from my eyes, and I from his. I am left with my kin and the rocking of the boat in the waves, and the knowledge that never again will I see my Golden One.

Chapter Twenty-Seven

Havardr Makes Plans

Standing with my mother's brother, I watch until I can no longer see Alimah on the boat that carries her away from me. My eyes can see no more; they are clouded by the moisture I cannot control. I could not persuade her to come with me and if I had forced her, she would never have forgiven me and would never have sung nor danced again. She might have gone to meet her ancestors like the song birds who cease singing when wrongfully captured. They languish until they cease to be.

I am already making plans to come back to her, back to her and to my child that I know she is carrying. Her body changed in that obvious way, swelling and softer, her small breasts more tender. When I came into her, I was careful, more careful than I thought I ever could be.

When I return to her, it will be forever. I have many strong brothers who can lead and protect our people. The woman with whom I am mated can be the mate of another strong warrior. She has not captured my heart, nor have I captured hers. I will not give up Alimah. This is not a final good bye, but only until we meet again. Maybe I can persuade some of the roaming ones to come with me and we can live like Alimah's kin do: selling, trading, living by our wits in the midst of great change. Her kin are honorable, that I have seen. I can live with and then help protect them. Perhaps even lead them.

Her uncle Bakiri told me the name of him who desires Alimah and wishes her for his own. A valiant warrior who is destined to be a leader of her kin. I must return before he takes advantage of my absence to mate with her and bind her to him with duties and affection, and other children. I must move quickly to reclaim her and our child.

Her body changed as the weeks passed by. I saw and understood. We talked softly at night, and I could not disagree with what she said about coming with me to my land where the water is so hard that it can be walked upon.

Alimah had sadly told me what was in her heart. "If I came with you, I would be seen as an outsider. Both because of where I come from and because of my gifts. Not all peoples cherish those like me. And our child would be a rival to your other mate's children. Our child would not be accepted. And when you went travelling, what would become of us, without you to protect us? If you were sent too soon to be with your ancestors, what would become of your child? What would become of me? My heart is torn, but I must stay here with my kin. I will continue to use my gifts and if our child has gifts, I and my kin will be sure to cherish them. We are safer here. I will tell stories of you, perhaps Dalil who has the magic with words will help me make up stories about you, so that you are never far from us."

I accept. I know she will be sought as the mate of someone worthy, for she is lovely and valiant. I would not want her to go through her life alone. If it is not fated that I can return and reclaim her, who is my heart, I must not go through my life alone. I must make many fine children with another. But, when it is time to go to my ancestors, I will be remembering her hand in mine, her body with mine, her voice raised up in song. Perhaps she will be there on the other side.

If I cannot return to her.

Chapter Twenty-Eight

Alimah Journeys to the Remains of Ugarit

Up the Great Green Sea we sail. The first several days I want to sit quietly and weep, but I know that is unworthy. The brothers need my help to sail, to prepare food, to lighten the journey for all of us.

We make good time. The weather stays clear—no sudden storms disrupt our journey. Arudara and Diripi tell me stories of their growing up together. They tell stories of Petros the Younger and Salama, his new mate. I learn much about my people, and about those I journey with. I thought I had known these things, but then I was a child with a child's understanding. Now I was no longer a child, and I hear the stories with different ears.

After several days of quiet, new songs come to me that I try out on my small audience. They like them. Arudara works on a few pieces of jewelry, I sing my songs, and Diripi looks content to be back on the sea where he belongs. He pilots us with his head lifted, seeming to smell when the wind will change. He reads the birds in the air, and the sea creatures—both those who cavort around us and the fish who provide us with meals. The sails slap against the booms, the wind whistles in the sails, the waves make a thrumming noise against the hull of our tidy craft. At night we anchor in a secluded cove and enjoy the sounds of the wind in the trees and grasses that guard the shore. We hear the cries of the hunting birds, sometimes the screams of the prey they find. It is the sounds of the night on land. The sounds mean that we are not known to the human predators who have caused us such troubles. Dates from the trees we can see from our tidy boat nourish us. Sometimes we trade something for loaves of sustaining bread in the small towns nestled in the coves. Those who give us food are wary, for the Great Destruction has made all wary.

We approach Ugarit, the place that is no more. As is the way with our kin, we all grow quiet, for much of our history is bound up in that destroyed city. When we reach the area there is one figure who awaits us with war mares.

I see it is The Bedouin, he who is a blood brother to Petros the Wise, he who is so taken with Serena. He hails us as we come ashore.

"I have been sent by Petros the Wise to meet you," he says.

I rub the war mare's soft nose; she snuffles her hot breath on my neck.

"I will escort you back to your kin." He eyes me. When last he saw me, I was a child, almost grown, but a child. I hold myself differently now. I have experienced much and it shows.

"We thank you for your courtesy," Diripi says. "Have there been new troubles?"

The Bedouin looks at me uncertainly. When last he saw me I was inexperienced in troubles.

Diripi sees and answers the unspoken question. "Since you have last seen her, Alimah has had many adventures, and learned much of the ways of the world. She has been tracked by evil ones who wanted her gifts. At the school she was a target of those not as gifted as she. There were dangerous times when she had to ride for long days to evade those who would either harm her or hold her for ransom. She was the one who figured out why those at the school were dangerous to her. She has the right to know of new troubles."

The Bedouin's stern face relaxes and he says under his breath, "Just like Serena."

Diripi and Arudara both proudly agree with him. "Yes, just like Serena."

"We will take you to my people first, to make sure it is safe to restore you to your kin. We hear of those who chase after the bright stones, making inquiries about you, Arudara, and you, Alimah." The Bedouin pauses and then continues, "Petros the Wise thought it would be safest to bring you gradually back to your kin. By that time it should be obvious from where the danger comes."

He does not speak the word, but I believe Petros the Wise will take care of those who wish us harm, either by guile, which he prefers, or by destroying them if he has to.

I will sleep under the stars of the desert and dream of my Golden One, whom it might be wise to forget, but whom I do not wish to forget. I will live in the tents with the women and children, which I am not used to. I will be safer there than in a tent alone. I can always sing softly to myself, if the women and children do not want to hear my songs.

Arudara gives me a long look. He will have his bright gems with him, so maybe he will be able to continue with his work. Or maybe not. He says, "Until we meet again."

Diripi says to me, "Until we sail together again on the Great Green Sea, Alimah."

I have been through so much upheaval since staying in the Land of the One River that I can no longer be frustrated by small things. Having killers come after me, having evil people come after me has taught me to react calmly to that which used to make me shout.

As I say goodbye to Diripi and Arudara I think of the many I have said "fare thee well" to: Bakiri, my beloved uncle, my protectors and guards in the Land of the One River, and my Golden One. At the thought Havardr, I can hardly keep the tears from coursing down my face. How I wish for him! His babe makes fluttering movements. My heart has not grown used to leaving he who has been my love.

Chapter Twenty-Nine

Alimah Rides with The Bedouin

Traveling along the ancient trails with The Bedouin, I think back to the time, not so long ago, when I travelled not only with The Bedouin but also with Petros the Wise, Serena, Dalil, and Kaliq. I was a still a child then, with a child's understanding. I was used to being protected and knew not how to think or act for myself. I have learned much.

The Bedouin and I talk as we ride along, remembering the long journey we have made in each other's company. I ask him what he knows of our companions and if all of them are well. He tells me what he knows. I hear again of Dalil's coming into his gift of storytelling and of the girl, Leila, now his mate and his partner in storytelling.

"The stories are marvelous, Alimah. All those who listen to them are quiet, as if their revered ancestors come alive before them. You will enjoy them."

I reply, "It will be a pleasure. Dalil is a fine man, I am so happy he has found the one who is right for him."

I must look sad, for The Bedouin said gently, "Alimah, your gifts are so great that you will find your way, too." He quiets and continues, "I am not of your kin, but I see how your gifted ones have hard times."

I look at him, and my lower lip quivers. "It is so hard to do the right thing. It is so hard to be true to my gifts."

The Bedouin looks straight ahead between the war mare's ears, focused on what I know not. "Serena said much the same, Alimah. You are very like her." His voice softens, "Serena the Wise is what she should be called."

"Thank you for that," I reply.

"The path you have chosen or your gifts have chosen for you may be a hard one. Your gifts set you apart and demand more from you than most of us realize. If ever you need a place of refuge, I will provide it for you." This is maybe the longest speech that I have ever heard from The Bedouin, for he is a man of the desert and of few words.

"Thank you. I hope I never have that need, but if I do, I will remember and come to you." I bow my head to him.

Chapter Thirty

Alimah With the People of the Desert

The Bedouin sets the pace. In places along the ancient trade route we ride briskly with few or no stops. I can tell by the demeanor of my guards that we are in dangerous territory. At times we slow our pace, perhaps in deference to my being with child. We sleep at night under the stars, or at least I sleep. I am aware of being guarded day and night. We leave the trail to go into the Great Desert where his people live. He reads the signs and know where we were going. We reach an oasis each night. I am relieved, although I have heard of the ways of those who live in the desert. Much time goes by until we reach the camp of his people.

We settle in. I sleep in the tent with the women, the children and the war mares. They find me strange but know that The Bedouin, much respected among his people, wants me treated well. I help with the children, and help with the cooking. In time, I start humming songs as I work, and then sometimes they burst out of my throat, to the amazement of those around me. Time goes by; my child grows larger and more insistent. It is more difficult for me to move. I awaken many nights with wet cheeks, after dreaming of my Golden One. The women I live among see and say nothing but make kind gestures. The children come and pat my hand to console me. Thinking not of the future, I live as in a dream. The tears come only in the night—by day I keep them hidden.

Petros the Younger and his mate Salama arrive one evening as the sky fades to dark blue and the stars become visible in the sky. They are greeted by the people of the desert as old friends, as indeed they are. Petros the Younger has fallen in love with the war mares and, truth be told, has fallen in love with the ways of wandering in the desert. He has tried to help those who need his clever hands—mainly the war mares and the women who come to the time to bring new life into this world. The desert peoples' lives seem to make them decline to try to help those in trouble giving birth, whether the valuable war mares or the not so valuable women. I know that Petros the Younger finds it difficult when he could have helped so many.

Our desert friends find Salama and her schemes to sell their brightly embroidered cloth more to their taste. Petros the Younger takes a close look at my swollen body and queries me.

"How many moons have gone by since your last flow?" he asks.

We are alone, yet I am not shy. I count on my fingers. "Seven. My time is not yet, Petros."

"I think it would be best if I am with you then. I have some skill," he says.

"I know. I think it would be best, too." We both know how dangerous the birthing of a babe can be. He looks at my small body and I can see that he is worried.

"Is it safe for me to be restored to the kin? I remain here for safety, only."

"Soon, Alimah. I must speak to The Bedouin. He may have heard rumors that I have not. I want to move you before very long, but not put you in danger."

"I leave it in your hands."

What else can I say? I can only wait and rely on others.

Chapter Thirty-One

Alimah and Salama Talk

Salama and I talk. She is as easy as Serena, her mate's mother, to talk to. I realize how much I need to talk to another woman. I tell her of Havardr, my voice growing soft as I describe our rides away from danger. I tell her of why I did not return with him to the land of bitter cold. Why I could not stay with him. Her face softens as she hears of my reasons and sees the sorrow those reasons bring to me.

"He said he would return for you?" she asks.

"Yes. But I cannot live my life thinking he will return, for he may never be able to. It could be he would change his mind and find he cannot leave his duty," I say, trying to keep my eyes dry.

"I think he wants to," she says with hesitation, her eyes shadowed.

"You have the far seeing sight, do you not?" I ask.

"Yes, but sometimes I just get fragments and not a clear picture."

Her hands are clenched. What is she seeing that is so disturbing? My Golden One returning to his ancestors? That I will never again see him? I look at her terrified.

"Calm down, Alimah. I see him through a mist; it is not clear. You have described him so clearly that perhaps that is what I am seeing."

People keep telling me not to worry. I get angry at all these well-meaning words. The father of my child is not here. I know that I may have difficulty birthing a babe because I am so small. I may not survive. My babe may not survive. And all they can tell me is to keep calm!

Salama sees my anger, which I cannot conceal, puts her hands over mine and says, "I will never again tell you not to worry. I will no longer tell you to stay calm. Forgive me. It won't happen again." She looks at me, pleads with me, tries to assure me of her understanding.

My anger subsides and I smile at her. I am glad that she is here. I am glad that she is one of the kin. We have been slowly walking for I can no longer walk swiftly. But if I do not move about I become cross. Under the high desert sky we talk quietly, although our words are not understood by those who know not our language.

She changes the subject. She asks, "How does Bakiri my kinsman?"

Relieved to be talking of a matter which does not hurt my very being, I say,

"He is learning how to care for the gifted ones. I believe I taught him much. Although at times when I answered him, I think he wanted to stomp and yell and say to tell him what I meant. I think working with the war mares was soothing for him after trying to figure me out." I hear the welcome laughter in my voice.

"I was a trial to him and he often lost his temper with me," Salama, her lips twitching and her eyes brimming with laughter, declares.

Much entertained, I reply to her. "He told me of it and is trying to change. It is hard on him. I think he tries to regard the gifted ones as particularly sensitive war mares who have to be treated very gently."

Salama laughs and laughs, until tears run down her cheeks—a sound that cheers me. I pause and then, holding tight to her hands, I join her in her laughter.

We pause in our walk, for my babe is stirring and making me uncomfortable. "I called him Uncle Bakiri. He is a good man and a smart man, so like Petros the Wise. We had many adventures. I can think of very few with whom I would trust myself. He is one." I am still smiling at Salama, ready to break out in laughter again.

Salama says quietly, "He is a good man and I tried his patience. He could not understand me. I am glad to hear that he is learning how to protect and cherish the gifted ones. Thank you for your love of him, for that is what it was."

"Yes, I learned to love many on this adventure," I answer.

"The Golden One?" she asks carefully.

"He will always be in my heart," I reply.

Chapter Thirty-Two

Alimah Waits

Petros the Younger and his mate, Salama leave. I am left here alone. Soon, they say, soon I will be taken back to the kin.

Petros the Younger has helped a war mare deliver a fine foal. Our hosts are not used to having the help in birthing. The elders do not like it, think it is wrong. Their ways are harsh. Those who cannot stay in one piece are left to die. Just like the herds of sheep or goats or the fleet creatures of the desert: keep up or die. Be born, climb to your feet immediately or you will be a predator's meal.

But under that broad sky filled with stars, beneath the shining moon, it seems a good way to live. The greed and anger and hidden lusts that are so vexing in the Land of the One River are not here. All is simple.

Every night I dream of my Golden One. I cling to those dreams because in the daytime there is no one to remind me of him. I am afraid that as the days follow I will forget what he looks like. I remember sailing away from him and seeing him grow smaller and smaller and finally disappearing in the mist. Perhaps he is disappearing in the mist even now, though his child and mine grows more active every day.

What will my kin make of all this? My heart lurches at the thought.

I stay in the place of the desert peoples. In the Land of the One River I had become accustomed to bathing at least twice a day, accustomed to the pristine feel of my skin and hair. Here in the desert, I grow accustomed to never bathing, to not even missing it. The smells of the cooking, so different from what I was accustomed to, the smells of living with the war mares, and the smells of unwashed bodies do not offend my nostrils.

The men go out on raids on the war mares, coming back with herds of goats as prizes from their combat. Never did they war over the bright stones, as those in other places do. If they can also capture fine war mares that pleases them.

I long to return to my kin and am becoming more and more restless. My child grows larger and more active, and I am ready to leave. The Bedouin has left on some duty or other and I feel even more alone. I have no one to talk to who has any idea of what my life has been. They are not unfriendly but know not what is in my heart. I wait.

One of those with whom I live watches and before I can see anything he knows that riders are approaching us. I stare and stare. Among these riders are The Bedouin and Kaliq. I want to hide, but cannot. I face what must be faced.

Chapter Thirty-Three

Kaliq Comes For Alimah

Kaliq takes me aside from the others. Most would not understand what he is saying, but still he takes me aside, for which I am grateful.

"When is your child due?" Kaliq asks.

"Soon," I reply. The women among the Bedouin have seen the signs and know that I am with child. They do not know my language and I speak haltingly in theirs. It needed not language, however, to see the obvious.

"Were you forced?" Kaliq's eyes grow hard at the thought.

"No," I reply.

"Who was it?" Kaliq persists.

"It was Havardr, Kaliq. He was a student at the school. Enemies stalked him and then me. The Bedouins took us from place to place to preserve our lives. Violence surrounded us." I am unable to continue. The words cannot come out of me.

"Why is he not here with you?" *Does Kaliq sound accusing?* I can hardly recognize the sound of his voice.

"He had to return to his people who live far away where the water turns solid from the cold." I am turning cold. His questions are relentless.

"Why didn't he take you with him?" Kaliq does not look friendly.

"He wanted to. I refused to go with him." I am near tears. I have never seen how stern Kaliq can be.

"Why?" He has not touched me, either in anger or in any other way. I start shivering.

"I could not leave my kin." I stop shivering and almost spit the words. "I could not leave you."

At these words, Kaliq looks surprised. The implacable look is gone; back is the Kaliq whom I know.

"Even though you carry his child." His voice is softer.

"It is my child, too. I could not leave my kin, I have duties here. Here, there are people who have known me since I was a babe. I would always be a stranger in a strange land with no one to defend me, no one to care if I lived or died."

"Ah." Kaliq looks at my face, at the sadness.

"He wanted me to return with him to his people in the far away land where the water turns solid. Their men of power can have many wives. I would not go with him, for I would no longer be able to make songs or dances. I could not leave my people." I quietly add, "Or you." I wonder if he believes me.

"Did he know of the child?" Kaliq asks.

"Yes." I reply, my voice wobbling. I remember how our joining changed as my body changed, how he was very careful with me. I remember how he refused to say good bye, said we would meet again.

Kaliq softly touches my shoulder. I am surprised at the comfort that small gesture brings to me.

I wonder if he will be willing to have me as his mate, since I have lain with another and carry another man's child. Kaliq does not know that I was attracted to Havadr even before danger fell upon us. I do not want to tell him, but I will. My honor demands it. Kaliq, whom I have loved forever, it seems. Whom I have known longer than Havardr. If Kaliq is still willing, can I return to a familiar life, familiar hardships? I no longer know what I wish for. Can I lie with him as I did with Havardr? What of my dreams?

The child grows larger and more demanding. Dancing is difficult. Songs seem to stop in my throat, I cannot sing with joy or even sadness when my heart is so torn. I dream of Havardr at night, dream of his large body covering mine, dream of sky- shadowed eyes on me, dream of coming out of my dreams to awake in his arms, with him embedded inside of me. My heart seems to have gone with him. But how can I leave all that I have known to be his mate in that far away land? Who would protect me and my child when he was gone, or if he went to meet his ancestors? I know how other peoples choose their leaders. My child would not be chosen but would have to make his way on his own, and perhaps be in more danger because of his mother and his father.

I know from conversations with Serena and from what I have seen that with some men it matters who a woman has lain with or has had children with. With others it does not. I do not know which kind Kaliq belongs to. His face is quiet. He has learned much in his time with Petros the Wise, has learned to conceal his thoughts. I know from our journey together that that look means that he is thinking and scheming. His intelligent eyes sharpen as he gazes upon me. He sees something of my turmoil. More, perhaps, than I know.

"Do not fear, Alimah. I will guard you well on our journey to the kin. I will take care of you." He covers my trembling hands with his own. I relax, for the Kaliq that I knew before has returned to me.

Chapter Thirty-Four

Kaliq and The Bedouin Speak

"She is so small that she might have trouble bringing that child into the world. When I spoke with Petros the Younger he was concerned. That is why I am here to return her to our kin. I know it is late, but I dare not wait any longer. The trail is clear; now is the time to leave. Will your people object?"

"No, Kaliq. They will not understand, but she is not one of us, so they will not object. You are uneasy?"

"Her heart has been torn asunder. So yes, I am uneasy."

The Bedouin's fierce eyes and grim mouth signal what he will ask next, the same question that Kaliq has asked. "Was she forced?" Manners have kept him from asking the question of Alimah. He knows that her heart is torn but dares not ask more.

"No, she says not," Kaliq replies.

"Who is the father?" Then, The Bedouin's face stills in understanding. "It was Havardr, wasn't it? I have been told of how they rode and rode to escape danger in the Land of the One River. Alimah and Havardr were thrown together

131

during all of this. My kin recognized what was happening between them. But they were already aware of each other before those long journeys to escape danger. This I heard from my people."

Kaliq nods his head. "Yes, I have heard the same. And heard the same from Alimah. It started during their time together at the school. When danger came upon them, and they spent the days and nights together, never knowing if they would see the light of day unharmed, they could no longer resist."

Kaliq quiets, remembering the days when Serena and The Bedouin were trapped in one small room. They faced torture and a long, horrible death. Together they managed to evade that fate. Kaliq remembers the looks on their faces when rescued, and the subtle looks that bound them together after the rescue, before Lukenow came and reclaimed his mate and mother of his children and took her away on his tidy boat. Kaliq suspects that The Bedouin and Serena came close to lying together in the way of a man and a woman. A few more days and perhaps they would have. If they had partaken of the red seeds that dim the mind with dreams, perhaps it would have happened no matter what their wishes.

Kaliq wishes that Petros the Wise or Serena were here to help him understand what to say to Alimah. He would like to fold her in his arms, but the babe, the babe that is not his, would get in the way. She is so large that he can no longer get his arms around her. If he had insisted that she come with him when he left the Land of the One River, none of this would have happened. Sadly, he thinks again.

It is never wise to force the gifted ones to do something they desire not. Something hurts in them, and they can no longer use their gifts.

Kaliq thinks further. Havardr tried to persuade Alimah to return with him to his home far away, but she refused. He may have thought to force her and then, did not.

It is my duty to take care of her, he thinks. *It is my pleasure to take care of her, for she needs me, needs my strong hands and wits. She smiles no longer, her face is thin, her delicate arms are even thinner than usual.* He curses Havardr to himself, for not taking better care of Alimah and restraining himself from knowing her body.

He stops himself. The Bedouin has told him of what he heard about the tumult in the Land of the One River. Perhaps they did all they could. Arudara and Diripi who have returned told him also how confused and dangerous it was with villains chasing Havardr and Alimah for their beads and knowledge of the trade routes. *Would I have refrained from knowing her in the way of a man to a woman in the midst of all that danger and terror? Would I have taken her in my arms and celebrated life with her? Yes, I would have.*

What to do now? His quiet self knows the answer. Take care of her, take care of her and the babe. Just as Lukenow took care of Serena when Sardow went to meet her ancestors. Took care of Serena when she had been hardly used during her captivity, took care of her when she became Arudara's milk mother, took care of her and had many fine children with her.

Alimah is mine, he thinks to himself. *I will take care of her and her babe.*

Chapter Thirty-Five

Kaliq and Alimah Journey to the Kin

As Kaliq and I prepare to leave our friends, he looks at me, then looks at the war mare standing so close to us, and murmurs softly so that none can hear. "I understand." He looks as if he has decided something—probably to do with me.

The babe takes that moment to kick me, so hard that I gasp. The babe reminds me that I cannot throw myself into Kaliq's arms. I will not fit.

"Your time is near?" he asks, although he knows the answer.

"Yes." *So near that I must return to my kin. It will be safer there.*

He eyes soften as he looks at me. So much is understood between us—so much that need not be said. Better to leave it unsaid. It is a road we cannot go down. Every step down my difficult trail is hard. I wish for Havardr but cannot leave my kin and what I think is my duty, both to the kin and to my gifts. Most of all, I cannot leave Kaliq, for I am bound to him. I have put aside my childhood, put aside the easy choices of childhood. I put my hand in his. It is my pledge to him.

"I will escort you back to the kin, Alimah. There is much danger now, and I and my men will return you to safety. We will protect you. Do not worry." Kaliq and his certainty ease my heart. My hand remains in his warm one. He brings my fingers to his mouth and caresses them.

We leave the next morning. A long day in the saddle is hard, even though we stop more often than we would if I were not large with child. Finally, when I droop and can no longer conceal how weary I am, we stop for the night at an oasis known only to the desert dwellers. The babe pummels me from inside. I go to sleep without eating, almost without speaking. My speech slurs as I try to thank Kaliq for taking care of me. He smiles at me and helps me down to sleep with my head against the war mare. I barely say anything before sleep claims me.

I awake drenched and groaning as the moon shines. Kaliq is by my side immediately. "Alimah."

I gasp, "The babe is coming." I hold on to his wrist, for the pains are great.

"There are no women with us to help, but you know that I have taken care of war mares," he says gravely, as he puts up a tent over us for shelter. The other men are quiet, on guard against any wanderers in the night. A small fire is built up to provide light for Kaliq. I know it is dangerous to give birth out here, but there is nothing I can do. The men will protect me against stray predators who walk on either two feet or four. Kaliq will protect me, will use his clever hands to help me and the babe.

I grip Kaliq's arms with my hands, grip with all my might. I try to not groan or call out but I have no control over that. My body will not let me be quiet. I wonder briefly if my cries will attract the dangerous roamers in our world. He gives me something to bite down on to stifle the sounds. I grip his arms and would not be surprised if I drew blood. He lets me hold on to him until the moment he goes to catch the babe as it emerges, squalling and covered with blood. He knows what to do: the war mares have taught him well. I pant with relief and hold out my arms for the quiet child that he has tenderly wrapped.

"He is a fine child, Alimah. Strong and handsome."

I have no time to think of anything but this new child to love and protect. I wish that Havardr were here but he isn't and never will be. Kaliq is here. His catching my babe as he emerged from my body makes our connection stronger. I catch the edges of a dream, catch the edges of something that eases my heart, eases the desolation that has overcome me: that Havardr is far away and I will never see him again.

Kaliq looks at me with softness in his eyes. He says, "We will rest a day and then move on, if you are strong enough. Rest, Alimah, rest. All is well." The night has lifted and the rays of the sun on this new day shine down on us. My son's tiny fingers are wrapped around Kaliq's strong ones. I look down at my babe and he looks back at me with eyes the color of the sky. The fuzz on his head is the color of gold, shining in the new day. I put my hand over theirs.

I can only smile as I fall into a deep, healing sleep—for my "Gold from the North" is well-protected by Kaliq. We are safe.

CAST OF CHARACTERS

Thutmose: Master sculptor to the Pharaoh Akhneaten
Hasna: Thutmose's beloved, gifted in languages

Abba: Master craftsman with whom Hasna takes refuge
Yunai: Abba's son; master negotiator and salesman
Arina: Abba's daughter; Hoval's beloved
Hoval: Son of Thutmose and Hasna; gifted in gems and gold

Some of the children of Arina and Hoval:
Petros: Warrior and protector; met Thutmose and grew up around Hasna
Sardow: Gifted in pottery and frescoes; has the far-seeing eye
Serena: Gifted in languages, disguises and the telling of stories
Lukenow: Man of the sea from Crete; bonded with Sardow before they grew into their adult bodies

Arudara: Only child of Lukenow and Sardow; beauty maker in gems
Diripï: Child of Lukenow and Serena; a man of the sea
Little Petros: Child of Lukenow and Serena, born warrior and healer
Little Sardow: Child of Lukenow and Serena, child of beauty

Salama: Distant kin from the Land of the One River

Nakhti: Salama's brother, also from the Land of the One River

Bakari: Head of the kin in the Land of the One River

The Bedouin: Blood brother to Petros the Wise and the kin

Dalil: Son to Petros the Wise; gifted in assuming the personae of others

Leila: Rescued by the kin, mate to Dalil

Kaliq: Cousin to Dalil, gifted with daggers as well as strategy

Alimah: Gifted in song and dance

The Golden One – Havardr: A warrior from Scandinavia

Kadem: A protector from the kin

Fahim: A protector, son an Egyptian man who bred the war mares

Menes: A protector, son of Bakiri

GLOSSARY

Land of the One River - Egypt

Land of the Two Rivers - Mesopotamia

Land of the Bull Dancers - Crete during the Minoan civilization

The Great Green Sea - the Mediterranean

Gold of the North - Baltic amber, as valuable as diamonds from later times

Cuneiform script: Wedge-shaped system of writing using a stylus on clay tablets. Originating in Sumer, it spread across Bronze Age civilizations using many languages. Used for diplomatic business (treaties, correspondence) as well as for everyday trade and commercial transactions which were essentially business contracts. Scribal schools were established in the region. The script ceased to be used and was replaced by alphabetic systems of writing and became extinct. In modern times the remaining clay tablets have been a treasure to archeologists.

Arabian horses: In the period of this story the horses were the property of the Bedouin and the mares were prized in warfare. The best stallions were kept for breeding. In modern times, the Arab horses are prized for their beauty, stamina and good natures.

Bedouin: Desert nomadic peoples, who left no written records.